SHERBROOKE S

A collection of important Canadian reprints
edited by John Metcalf and John Newlove

From a Seaside Town

Norman Levine

The Porcupine's Quill, Inc.

CANADIAN CATALOGUING IN PUBLICATION DATA

Levine, Norman, 1923-
  From a seaside town

(Sherbrooke street: a collection of reprints of
modern Canadian classics)
Rev. ed.
ISBN 0-88984-170-5

I. Title. II. Series.

PS8523.E87F74 1993   C813'.54   C93-094816-5
PR9199.3.L48F74 1993

Published by The Porcupine's Quill, Inc., 68 Main Street, Erin,
Ontario NOB ITO with financial assistance from The Canada
Council and the Ontario Arts Council. The support of the
Government of Ontario through the Ministry of Culture,
Tourism and Recreation is also gratefully acknowledged.

Distributed by General Publishing Co. Ltd.,
30 Lesmill Road, Don Mills, Ontario M3B 2T6.

Readied for the press by John Metcalf.
Copy edited by Doris Cowan.

Originally published by Macmillan and Co Ltd,
London, England, 1970.

Cover is after a photograph by Sam Tata.

Typeset in Trump Mediaeval, printed and bound by the
Porcupine's Quill. The stock is acid-free Zephyr Antique Laid.

To Margaret

Chapter One

WHEN A FRIEND from childhood met Emily for the first time he drew me aside and said: 'Clear out. She'll only drag you down.'

I didn't say anything.

At that time we were married four years and I could still be annoyed by some of the things she did. She left cups and saucers – on the table, in the kitchen, on the draining board, or jars in the cupboard – half way over the edge so that they fell. She left the tops off jars or put them on and didn't screw them down. I was always going around after her moving things away from the edge. I don't know why she was like this. Perhaps it was her shyness. On the telephone,* unless it was somebody she knew, she kept saying 'please'. And, like shy people, she had no small talk and came out with truthful but embarrassing things. She was also superstitious. If she saw a magpie she tried to find another. If there was a rainbow she'd say you mustn't point at it. She threw spilled salt over her shoulder, banged her elbows, put down to the full moon when she was on heat. There is nothing graceful about her, I thought, screwing down the white top on the Maclean's toothpaste tube. Yet the first thing you would have noticed about her as she walked in the street was the nice way she carried herself.

'You know,' she said, 'I think we see a little too much of each other.'

'Maybe. But I'd rather be with you than anyone else in this town.'

We had not long returned from a small party. It was the first party we had been invited to for over a year. I danced with the hostess (a resentful woman who married late in life) then found myself listening to the owner of a bric-à-brac shop who confided how miserable he had been since his wife left him. I saw the chair beside Emily was empty. I got away from the bric-à-brac man and sat down beside her.

She has this little girl's voice. Strangers who phoned, if she answered, would say to her: 'May I speak to your mother?'

'I think you're the best looker here,' I said.

She smiled.

Sitting in our living-room – in front of the open fireplace, it was banked and gave off a good heat – the Sunday papers on the carpet at our feet.

'I was bored at the party,' I said. 'Did it show?'

'Not to the others, but I knew.' She put down a section of a paper. 'Something odd happened at the party. I had to go upstairs and I didn't bolt the door. I forgot we weren't at home. Then this man walked in. Just as I was getting up. I don't think he saw anything. But I couldn't look him in the face all evening.'

She blushed as she spoke.

I visualized the scene. Then began to change it.

Emily got up. 'Would you like tea or coffee?'

'No. Let's go to bed.'

'What makes you randy all of a sudden?'

'You,' I said.

She went into the kitchen, set the table for tomorrow's breakfast. I put two empty milk bottles out, bolted the front door. She banked the back kitchen stove, brought the cat's box in. I went and put our youngest, Rebecca, half-asleep, on the toilet. Then waited in bed.

After twelve years of married life we knew our positions in bed as we did around the kitchen table.

I slipped out of her.

'Where's the towel?' she said.

I reached over and got the towel. She wiped her groin. Then she gave me the towel. I tried to wipe the wet parts of the sheet. In the end we pulled the sheet so neither of us would have the wet part.

'That was good,' she said.

She lay against my side, her head on my arm. Then it became uncomfortable.

'Shall I turn?' she asked.

She turned on her side, away from me, and I came close behind her so that we lay like a pair of stacked chairs.

'Goodnight love,' she said.

In the morning the children woke first. She got out of bed, made their breakfast, and saw them off. I waited until I heard 'Goodbye Daddy' then I began to get dressed.

At school that morning Rebecca wrote in her news book.

October 8. My daddy has gone to London. He is going to bring me a Rupert Booke a colouring booke for Ella and Martha something too.

I make these trips to London as often as I can. Sometimes it is on business. More often because I need to get away from here. And after four or five days I come back, the canvas bag filled with several loaves of rye bread (both dark and light), salami, hot dogs, cream cheese, herring, olives, a couple of pounds of chick-peas. I take off my coat. Emily brings me some coffee. I show her the delicatessen food.

'Let's go upstairs.'

She'd go but with a show of reluctance.

In the bedroom she would draw the curtain that daylight made pale yellow.

'What do you do in London that makes you always come back like this?' she said unzipping her dress in the back.

'It's all those pretty girls,' I'd say. Or, 'It's the train.'

Chapter Two

IN LONDON I stay with Albert. He has this ground floor flat in Kensington. His parents owned the whole building. They are now dead. And Albert was given this flat and the cook-housekeeper.

'Is your name Olga?' I asked her.

'I'm not Russian,' she said.

She doesn't hear too well and sometimes appears not to understand English. She's Czech. A small, energetic woman with freckles and grey hair. She attended his parents and now is there to look after him. But he's hardly there. He has taken a couple of rooms in Soho above a grocery store where, in complete disorder ('don't tell anyone about this') he is supposed to be writing. What he is writing I don't know. It must be the same thing he told me he was writing when I first met him eleven years ago.

'Sir,' Olga said. 'He's always making notes. Sunday. He goes to see his father's grave. We come away. He stops. Makes notes. He is driving the car – we are going somewhere – suddenly he stops the car, makes notes. In the middle of the street he stops and makes notes. Always making notes but never a book. He had this little girl.' (And here Olga said the name of a woman who is now well known as a novelist.) 'It was during the war. She didn't have much to eat. She would come to type his notes. I would make her something to eat. Then she has a book published. He ask her, how you make a book? She say you start somewhere and you go on from there. But he is only making notes.'

It is true. We can be having a conversation and he'll stop talking to write something down. But the only things I've seen of his published were letters to the papers to do with Jews. Albert has a thing about being a Jew. Olga told me, 'His mother want him to marry a Jewish girl. She say to him Albert there are many nice girls. Marry one. Bring up family. We'll help with the money. And when he is not in the house she ring up plenty of families who have girls. But then they all ask what does Albert do? Albert like this girl' (she points to a photograph on the mantel) 'she was not Jewish. His father did not want him to marry her. She married someone else.' (Another picture of the same girl in a white wedding dress with a man in a morning suit coming out of a church.) 'About a month after she married she was burned and is dead. I don't know why he goes so much the cemetery. He and his father always quarrelling. He loved his mother but with his father he quarrel. Now he goes every week to the cemetery.'

I sleep on a couch that is in a corner of the sitting-room. During the day the couch has a purple satin cover. The room is about sixty feet long and twenty feet high. The far wall has large windows, almost from floor to ceiling. And in front of the windows are heavy drapes that you move, like the windows, by pulling cords. But it's difficult to move in the room for it is overcrowded with furniture, mostly tables and chairs. You can tell the furniture has not been bought all at once. Nor was it arranged for anyone to sit down. And wherever you looked, stacks of books and magazines: on the tables, the sideboard, heaped against the walls.

'No one,' said Olga, dusting the room, 'can touch anything.'

The three typewriters, the tape-recorder, the record-player, the typing paper, clips, pens, envelopes, the road maps of Europe.

'He doesn't know what he has,' Olga said. 'He buys the same book twice.'

And the overcrowding, the haphazardness (kept spotlessly clean) only heightened the feeling that something was lacking. As if the accumulation of all the years was waiting for something to come along to make sense out of it.

Then there were the photographs. Several of his father and mother on top of the piano and on the mantel. Early ones, not the way I remembered the two, neatly-dressed, old people I met briefly one night on the way to see a French film at the Paris-Pullman. Albert introduced me. 'This is Joseph Grand, he is a writer.' 'Do you make a living at it?' his father asked. I didn't know then that Albert had sponged off him all his life. There were also numerous photographs of Albert. With a group in Army uniform, a belt of ammunition around his neck; with another Army group on a stage; with his brothers and sisters and their children on a beach in Devon; in France with a farmer and his wife and their daughter. It was as if he was accumulating evidence to show that, like other people, he too had a family, had friends.

'He is all muddled,' Olga said, sadly.

Then there is this business with Lily. I hadn't been up to London for a couple of months and when I did come up the first thing he tells me about is Lily. She has the basement flat below him. She is divorced. And he is enthusiastic about her. We all go out to the theatre and for a drink afterwards. Albert can't do enough for her. The next time I come up they have fallen out.

'What happened?'

'Oh,' he said, 'she had this niece staying with her and I accused Lily of being a lesbian. Now she tortures me. She has men back at night. And I can hear every time the bed creaks. I can't sleep. I listen. Or else I get mad and make a noise. I sing. Turn the bath – run all the taps. You won't speak to her?'

'No,' I said.

He let me have the flat for three weeks in July while he went on a car tour of Europe and North Africa. He sent me picture postcards. From France: 'Don't forget to put out the garbage on Tuesdays.' From Spain: 'Don't speak to Lily.' Another one from Spain: 'Your friends are welcome bring them back – but if anyone comes asking for me, don't let them in.'

In the time I've known him I now realize that I have been his longest friend. And I only see him when I go up to London. People use him. They stay at his place. They borrow small sums of money. They belong, like Albert, to the war and the early post-war years. Perhaps I do too. Although I'm not rooted in that time as much as he is. I had three years in the Air Force. While Albert spent five in the Army driving trucks and doing reviews and comic turns.

Now he's supposed to be running a business that his father left him. A man's clothing store in Shaftesbury Avenue. But he's hardly there. When they ring. It has to be make-believe on my part.

'Albert's not in – he's out – he'll ring back later.'

Meanwhile Albert has gone to France for a few days.

Another time I was staying with him, he said: 'I'm going to Edinburgh. Flying this morning. There's this girl at the Israeli Embassy going back to Israel. She said she'd like to see Scotland.'

NORMAN LEVINE

He got dressed in elegant sports clothes. Instead of looking dapper or sportslike he looked touchingly ridiculous. A middle-aged man dressed in young men's clothes.

When I got back to the flat that night his cases were in the hall and I could hear the bath running.

'Albert?'

'Yes.'

'What happened?'

'I'll tell you in a minute old boy.'

He came out, in his bathrobe, without his glasses he looked subdued. 'We got on the plane. I was feeling all excited. And she didn't want to talk. All the time we were in the plane she just read *The Times*. When we got to Edinburgh it was raining. I was fed up. I cancelled the hired car. I bought her a bit of jewellery for a present – I must be mad – and flew back.'

I met Albert not long after Emily and I were married. We were looking for a place to live in London. Albert heard from others that we were looking for a place and said he would help. He still has these sudden enthusiasms for other people's troubles. We were walking by Hyde Park Corner. It was evening. And a tall awkward-looking girl was standing in a bus queue with a tripod and a camera. Albert went up and said she couldn't go on a bus with all that equipment. He would get a taxi for her. But first he invited her to the flat. He gave her a drink. She had a habit of winking with her left eye that I'm sure she thought was seductive. She was a redhead and had brown eyebrows that didn't look real. She said she came from Putney and lived with her parents. Albert was full of suggestions. He would get her pictures in the *Sunday Times*, in the *Observer*. She said that all she did so far was work in the darkroom. In the end he lent her a book about photographers' agents, gave her a pound for a taxi. And never saw her again.

'Hullo old boy – you look exactly the same,' is the first thing he says when he sees me. But this time when I arrived he said: 'I must be getting old. It's about a month since I've had a woman.'

Later we went into one of those small dark restaurants off the Brompton Road. A girl and a boy were sitting next to us. Albert began to talk to them, found they were emigrating to Canada. So we all talked as we ate.

When we came back to the flat he said: 'I'm jealous of you.

13

The girl liked you. She doesn't want an old man.'

Next morning after breakfast he stood in the doorway, dressed in a dark suit, a dark coat, a dark homburg hat, holding a brown leather briefcase. 'I'm just off to the shop. I look like a real bourgeois, don't I?'

An hour later the phone rang.

'Hullo old boy.' He sounded out of breath. 'Any telephone calls for me?

'No,' I said. And I knew he had put the shop behind him.

I don't know what he does that matters in his life, except that he tries to complicate it. He has now decided to find out about his ancestors. He has this green map of Poland. I can hear him talking about it on the phone to his brother who owns a bra factory.

'Yes Monty, I have it here. *What's longitude?*'

He put the phone down, stared at the map. Two names were encircled north and west of Warsaw.

'It's a funny feeling looking at the map,' he said. 'To think my father began his life there.' And he disappeared from the room.

After a few minutes I called out.

'Albert, may I come in?'

'Yes old boy. I'll only be a minute.'

I saw him, in the other room, completely absorbed, writing something down.

Olga told me. 'I don't know where I am with him. One minute we are going to Poland for holiday by aeroplane. Then by car. Then by bus. Sir, I am too old to go by bus.'

'You know,' Albert said quietly in the disorder of the two rooms in Soho. 'I'm going to Poland. But I'm coming through Germany. There is a small town —' He stopped. 'Don't laugh. I want to go to this Nazi that got off. Knock on his door. Sometimes I wonder if I know myself.'

Chapter Three

ALTHOUGH I stay with Albert, the person I ring up next morning is Charles.

'I was just thinking of you,' he said. 'When did you get in?'

'Last night.'

'Can you come over?'

I like this part of London. Along the Old Brompton Road. The dark red brick, the outside flower boxes filled with geraniums, pink and red petals lying on stone steps. A 207A bus roars by the branch library on its way to South Kensington. I walk by the corner greengrocer where Emily used to shop. Cross at Queen's Gate. Here Emily pushed the pram on the sidewalk under the trees towards Kensington Gardens and I was in the large front room of a rented ground floor flat writing travel articles for *Vogue* and *Harper's Bazaar*. The serve-yourself delicatessen, the small dairy, the pleasant gloom of the window filled with harps. I turn into a cul-de-sac and walk over cobble stones.

Charles's door is painted a dull red. There is no door handle, just a button for a bell, and places where old locks have been. Near the roof are two windows with sacking for curtains.

I ring the bell.

The door opens enough to show Charles standing sideways. He has come down in stocking feet.

'How nice to see you.'

We go up the stairs. They are steep. I hold the thick rope on the side. At the top, large unprimed canvases against a partition. To the right, a small room, the door is open, it is his studio.

'How is Emily and the children?'

'Fine. She sends her love.'

We go to the left, to the kitchen. A gas stove, a plain wooden table against the wall, a couple of wooden chairs. At the far end a bath with bathroom scales beside it.

'How long is it since you were up?'

'Nearly four months. Some day I'll get us out of there.'

We sit by the wooden table. He offers me a Gauloise and we both light up. Then he puts on the kettle for some coffee.

'How's your work going,' I said.

'Much the same. Are you doing another book?'

'Yes.'

'I didn't like the last one.'

'Neither did I. I've lost interest in doing travel things. Have you a show coming up?'

'In November. In New York.'

'Will you go over?'

'The gallery want me to go. But I don't think I will.'

And I remembered his dealer, a former German refugee, saying, 'Charles, now that you earn more than the Prime Minister and the Archbishop of Canterbury, why don't you go and visit the United States?' 'My world is the other way,' Charles said, indicating Europe.

'I went to Connolly's sixtieth birthday party,' he said. 'I think it went on for a couple of days. Before going I read *The Unquiet Grave* and memorized a couple of passages hoping I'd be able to quote them to him. But when I got there I couldn't remember a thing. Are you all right for lunch?'

'Yes,' I said.

When Charles came into our lives it brought an element of glamour. At that time he wasn't as well known as he is today. But even then walking down the street with him was like walking with a popular film star. Once, while we were having lunch in the Lyons Steak House in the Brompton Road, a girl with an older man were on their way out. The girl stopped at our table.

'Charles Crater?'

Charles smiled and tilted his head up and said, 'Yes.'

'You probably don't remember,' the girl said, 'but we met at a party about a year ago.'

Charles continues smiling, as he always does when he is nervous.

I recognize the girl. A performer on children's television. She sings and plays the guitar. As soon as they had gone, 'Who is she?' Charles said, his voice lower.

I told him and what the girl did.

'Is she any good?'

This has always been one of his criteria with people: are they any good at whatever they do. His paintings now sell for two thousand pounds and over yet he continues to live in this small three-roomed flat with very few pieces of furniture. In the other room there is only a large bed with a brightly coloured bedspread – a rug that he brought back from Tangier.

A bedside table with a small record player, some records (Piaf, Brecht/Weill) and books (*King Lear*, Proust, a paperback of Nietzsche) a large glass ashtray. There is a settee, and opposite it a table. On the table a television set.

'That's new,' I said.

'I got it to try and keep me in at night. It doesn't.'

Otherwise few possessions. Charles has a thing about possessions. And continually gives things away. He has given me *The Goncourt Journals*, *The Letters of Van Gogh*, Painter's biography of Proust, Colette's *The Pure and the Impure*.

'What are you working on?'

'I'm doing some portraits but I've got nothing to show you. The gallery took them yesterday.'

I go to the small room to the right at the top of the stairs. A mixture of disorder ('but I know where things are') and neatness. Messages are painted on one white wall. Names and telephone numbers. A dentist's bill is stuck on marked paid. There are several empty tin cans (ordinary dessert fruit tins, they still have their brand labels and the bright pictures of pears and peaches) with his brushes neatly stacked in them. Behind them, on the wall, is an elliptical mirror and around the mirror the wall is full of brush strokes. On another wall (opposite to where the messages are) are reproductions of some of his paintings cut out of magazines. A man sitting in the nude, a lying down figure, several portraits. Until I saw Charles's portraits I had not noticed the colours of the face – the light greens, the pinks, the whites. I asked him once why he painted the flesh so much. 'Because I like the colours.' But then went on to describe seeing an expensively dressed woman walking by the meat department of Harrods. And the kind of connection this has for him. Against the wall are some canvases, their backs facing the room. In the centre, his easel caked with lumps of paint. And on the floor, in large untidy heaps, are all kinds of picture magazines – from Germany,* France, Italy, America, England – with pages torn out of them. Charles constantly searches through picture magazines looking at the photographs.

---

* *My uncle took me to Berlin in the twenties. It was very free. So anything went. 'Was it like Isherwood's Berlin?' I asked. 'He saw it as an English public schoolboy. The real thing was much more stark.'*

While I had another cup of coffee, another Gauloise, he shaved. He has a largish face, small light grey eyes. His eyes appear small because of the largeness of his face. When he sees you for the first time, or after an absence, he smiles and looks into your face as if there was no one in the world he so much wanted to see. It is a way he has. He excites himself with people and conveys that excitement to you. He can walk into a kitchen which may be in a bit of a mess with children running around, the breakfast things not cleared away, sit down and talk, and make you forget your surroundings. As he talks his face is continually changing expression. 'One goes through life,' he once told me, 'hoping to meet people with whom one can clarify.' But this charm and grace is one side of him. I remember another time when he came down to Carnbray to see us. I called for him at his hotel room. We were both invited to dinner at the Middletons'. The hotel room overlooked a sandy beach. He went to the window and looked down on the people on the beach. And he was full of contempt for the people below him breeding, for marriage as an artificial institution.

'I bet they're watching,' he said, looking in the mirror, by the open window, arranging a bit of hair to fall just right, 'and saying look at a queer doing his hair. Sometimes I wonder why I bother. It's just vanity. I'm all grey. If I didn't dye my hair you would see. What's the time?'

'Ten to twelve. Don't you wear a watch?'

'I've had many. But I can't keep them. They all get taken.'

We catch a taxi and go to Wheelers and have oysters and fresh salmon and wine. And Charles pays by cheque.

Sometimes we arrange to meet somewhere and he doesn't turn up. The first time it happened he said he would see me at his place at five. I waited outside the door, but he didn't come. Next morning I called. When he opened the door he said he had a hangover. And quickly put on a pair of dark glasses. Over coffee he said he had just got rid of some people he was drinking with yesterday.

'I'm glad they went, otherwise I'd have to get them and me drunk again. It's such a bore. I'm sorry about yesterday. But I just began drinking. There's a place off Shaftesbury Avenue. I met these two. They knew I could give them things they couldn't have. That's why they go there. But I must get down to work.'

In his company I have met a deep sea diver, a wealthy farmer, a Negro solicitor, an actor, a teacher, a photographer, some painters, but mostly working-class men.

'I like people who are physically and mentally tough,' he said. 'I don't think I'm physically very tough. But mentally I am.'

Once he told Emily. 'What do you like about people? Their youth. The kind of ambitions they have.'

He has a wide circle of acquaintances. 'I don't see much of Cameron,' he said, 'although we used to be great friends. He says I have said bitchy things about him. Probably I have. But then who can one say bitchy things about, if not your friends.'

When he comes down to Carnbray it is to get away from London and the kind of life he leads. But for us his presence is a high point in our lives. People I don't see all year phone up to ask if Charles is down. He will take Emily and me out to a good restaurant. Then go by himself for a ride on a bus across the moors. Or have tea in a crowded cheap café with lots of people about.

Once when he came down he saw our next door neighbour, Miss Benson, a spinster, washing her outside steps. He said Hello to her. Further down the road I told him how on Christmas Day we always ask Miss Benson to come in the house for a drink. She's a strict Methodist and doesn't drink all year except for this once when she'll have a sherry. When Emily went in to get her she found Miss Benson sitting at the table in the kitchen with bacon and eggs for her Christmas dinner looking miserable. She was waiting for a Christmas parcel from a friend in Canada. And it hadn't come.

'I've been alone at Christmas,' Charles said in his low flat voice.

Another time he was in the room when I was reading a bedtime story to the children. 'Happiness said the dark fairy —'

'What would a fairy know about happiness,' Charles interrupted.

He came to see me off at Paddington. There were about twenty or thirty young soldiers also waiting on the platform. They had just come off a train.

'What are you going to do afterwards?' I asked.

'I wouldn't mind going off with one of them,' he said. 'But I don't make a pass – unless I'm drunk.'

Just before the train pulled away. He took out several pound notes and put them into my hand. 'For the children,' he said and smiled.

Chapter Four

IN LONDON I see Albert and Charles. But here in Carnbray there is only Jimmy Middleton. We ring up each other, we meet in a pub and talk over drinks. Most of the people I've met down here don't belong – Jimmy does. Not only was he born here but so was his father (he inherited £50,000 from him) and his grandfather and great-grandfather. I helped Jimmy move into the nicest house I know in Carnbray. An all timbered house on the slope above the harbour. He has a tennis court, large trees – his children have made houses in them. And several greenhouses where his wife Esther – a small blonde who looks very self-contained – grows exotic plants. Jimmy is a marine biologist attached to a marine biology place some thirty miles up the coast. Once I went up with him and he showed me around his lab. He had a dredger working off shore bringing back samples of the seabed. Then he would try to find, 'my little beasties'. (I saw through his microscope something transparent, like a seahorse.) And plot their movements to see if they were in sufficient density for a new source of protein. Jimmy is forty-two. He has a swarthy face, a large forehead, and black hair with streaks of grey, that he parts on one side. He has broad shoulders. He is in good health and very strong. There is something about Jimmy that I put down to all those paintings of his ancestors on the walls. He's on several committees, a member of clubs. He pays his bills right away. He is a Christian, a believer. And he is entirely dependable. If he says he will be at a certain place, at a certain time, he is there. And he expects you to be there as well. He doesn't read much. I give him copies of the magazines with my travel pieces in them. But I only remember him making one literary comment. He thought *Lolita* a very profound and sad book. When he comes to the door he usually has a flower or something from their gardens for Emily. He likes Emily. But near the start he told me: 'Someone in your position ought to have married money.' Esther also comes from a stable middle-class family. She met Jimmy on a gold course. In the house she showed me an etching on the wall, one of her ancestors fighting with Wolfe on the Plains of Abraham.

Perhaps it is because he has this stability that Jimmy deliberately takes risks. He drives a fast car. And about three or four
times a year runs away from Esther and the kids and the large
house. The reason given is to attend scientific meetings and
lecture trips abroad. But he uses them as opportunities for sexual encounters. Perhaps because sex seems to have come late
into his life. When he returns the first thing he tells me is of
his latest conquest. The Swedish female translator he was
marooned with for three days in a ski-resort, he showed me
the rag doll ('our baby') she gave him when he left; Huguette,
the wife of a French civil servant he met in Amsterdam; a
dentist's wife in Brussels. We would discuss some new varia-
tion in sexual position. And the effect of using brandy, ice-
cream, or shaving-soap, on the cunt. Once when I had come
up for lunch to his place and we both had too much to drink
and we were on the lawn sitting in chairs by a rough wooden
table. He told me of his recent trip to Italy. He went to a village
in the mountains to see something about sewage. 'There was
this peasant girl. She had a goat with her. The girl insisted I
have the goat first. The goat went down on its front legs. All
the time it was enjoying it – its head was rolling from side to
side. Then I had the girl.'

Sometimes I think he exaggerates all his successes.

We watched Esther walk from one of the greenhouses,
across the neatly cut lawn, to the house.

'She'll have me in the end,' Jimmy said.

Chapter Five

THAT'S THE WAY the last five years have gone by. Living in Carnbray, going off for short trips to do the travel articles. Every two years putting the travel pieces together for a book. And coming up to London whenever I feel the need to snap out of the lethargy I get into down here.

Then something unexpected happened. A magazine I counted on taking an article a month folded and I lost £960 a year direct and another three hundred from syndication rights. Six weeks later in the morning's mail there was a brown envelope from the bank with my used cheques and a statement saying I was down to £5 8 6d.

I tried magazines that I never wrote to before. Then waited to see what the postman brought. I found the whole day centred around the postman coming. I'd get up early and wait anxiously until I saw him in the street opposite. Then stand by the window, to the side, so he wouldn't see me. I watched him as he worked the street opposite, before he came here. And hid until I heard the release of the letter slot. I got to know all the postmen's habits. Who was fast. Who dawdled. Who talked. And if no money came it meant having to go out and think what I could do about lunch when the children came back from school.

I would try to get Emily to go to the Co-op, see the manager, say I would pay next week, could she have an order? But she wouldn't go. We owed them £26. In the end I went again. He said I could have another pound's worth of groceries but that would be the last time. I went around picking up things from the shelves. It was important to have something like a tin of salmon, a can of peaches, for our morale. And I came back, carrying the groceries in the overnight bag that I used for the London trips. The children were at the front window. They came running out of the house. Only later did I realize, by the inertia, just how much nervous energy was expended in these sorties.

It was in these circumstances that when Emily was offered a part-time teaching job in the country school near here she took it. And things began to change.

She now got up at seven and, after making the children's breakfast, walked the two miles to the school. She came back at half-past twelve. This meant I got lunch for the children.

In the afternoons she would do the washing, make the beds, tidy the house. And with her working the children were not as quiet as they once were when I was up here at the typewriter. We waited for her monthly cheque of some twenty pounds. And lived on that. And the occasional acceptance from an old article – by not paying the rent, by putting off paying the electricity, the gas, until threatened with disconnection. And for being in these circumstances she punished me in her own way. She wouldn't fuck.

At night I would come to bed and feel the hot water bottle near my feet with her feet on it. I would put my legs over hers, then put my hand on a breast. No response. Just the sound of the alarm clock from the floor muffled in a towel. I would kiss her eyes, sometimes they were wet. I would get on top of her. But her head would be turned away, her legs close together.

'You haven't brushed your teeth,' she said.

In a temper I'd get out of bed, find my clothes, put them on, go downstairs. Determined that tomorrow I would leave the house.

But tomorrow I would try to please her by getting a half-pound box of chocolates for her. (I know it was with the money she earned.) And that evening, after all the kids were in bed, and we sat on the settee watching TV I put out my hand on her thigh and felt something – suspender belt. I begin to stroke. And I think things are going to be fine. I suggest that we go to bed early. I say I'll do the back-fire. So she can be in bed first. And get a bit warm. (She's not interested if she's cold.) I stand in the bedroom in the dark with the light from the door opening – take off my jockey shorts, so she'll get the message. But it's no use.

The mornings go by fairly quickly. There is something to do. Clean the grate. Empty the ashes. Make the new fires, bring in coal, tidy up after the breakfast things have been cleared away. Make myself a cup of instant coffee. Listen to the news bulletins on the half-hour on the battery radio. Shave. Then around 11:30 get things ready for the children's lunch. At 12:15 get things ready for Emily's. Lay the table. Fill the kettle with water (the small saucepan for her boiled egg) bring out the bread and butter. By 12:30 light the gas.

I hear the front door. She comes in and asks: 'Any post?'

'Only a postcard for Martha saying to write to the four people whose names are on the card and she'll get 250 postcards back in twenty days.'

And there isn't much conversation left.

She has her egg and tea and some bread and butter. As I do, or a kipper if it's about. I listen to the sound of her breathing while she's eating. For some reason it irritates me. I make myself scarce by going upstairs into this room. And here I have to go through the afternoon. It's worse if Emily sees me doing nothing. I go to this room and close the door and type. I'll do a list of where I have things out. When I sent them. When I sent them reminders. What payments I expect to come in. And to Emily the sound of the typewriter meant I was working. I was trying. While we waited for the days to go by and for her to get the monthly cheque.

When the kids didn't want to eat the baked beans, the sardines, the macaroni and cheese, the minced meat – she said.

'Why do you think I'm working? You wouldn't have anything to eat if I wasn't working.'

And I would get up and leave the table.

Or she would come up here and ask. 'Can I have a little money?'

'Why don't you take a look in your purse. I left you a pound and some change.'

'I'm going to spend every penny of it on myself,' she said sharply.

She went down the stairs slamming the door behind her. She always slams doors when she is angry with me. It's her protest at being in a rented house she doesn't like, in a place she doesn't like.

When it rained and we didn't have the three-and-six for a taxi she would have to walk in the rain. She put cardboard in her shoes. But her feet were wet when she came back.

The headmistress thought she came back to teaching because of some vocation. 'How can I tell her I'm only doing it for the money. And what money? A babysitter in London gets more than I do.'

If things went wrong. Like Ella falling and I had to take her to the hospital for an x-ray on her wrist. Emily said, 'If I was home this wouldn't have happened.' Or when the cat died. 'If I was home I would have called the vet.'

In the evenings, though we were in the same room, we hardly talked. We borrowed books from the library but we brought them back unread. I tried to pass the time playing solitaire on the dining-room table. She watched television. I made side bets with myself. If this game comes out I'll have an acceptance. This week. This month. Make a trip to London. Make a trip somewhere else. Emily will fuck tonight. The next woman I'll marry will be a twelve-foot Amazon. A three-foot dwarf?

'What bet are you having tonight?' she asked.

'If I'll earn enough money to get us out of here,' I said.

'But you like being poor,' she said.

Was she right? Perhaps I do. Perhaps this is one of the things that has held us together.

I continued to play solitaire.

Sometimes I would stay downstairs and not come up until after midnight.

'Why are you so late?' she said as I entered the room.

'I thought you would be asleep.'

'I can't go to sleep.'

I would get undressed and come into bed beside her. She would take my hand in hers as if going for a walk and in a matter of minutes she would be asleep.

And when something did come. Like a cheque from an old travel piece on Carnbray that was reprinted in a German magazine, Emily would get a chicken from the butcher. And she would fuck that night. And I would remember those other nights and vow never to let us get into that position again.

In the afternoon I'd ask her to come upstairs.

She did.

I'd brush my teeth. She brushed hers. Sex had to start with a brushing of teeth – it was an obsession with her – our mouths had to smell of toothpaste.

'You're lucky,' she said undoing her bra. 'If you had a job you wouldn't be able to do this. Not many people can do this in the afternoon.'

Afterwards, I saw her pulling up her dark suspender belt. I made a pass with my hand at it as she wriggled out of the way and pulled it up.

'Why are you such a puritan?'

'Because I've got such horrible underclothes,' she said. 'Ask a silly question.'

But a week later the money ran out and we were back to the old routine.

'I don't want to play any more,' Emily said. 'You are suddenly tired of it all. You want another game. I don't mean *you*. I mean life.'

Then I hated coming up here, to sit at the desk, look at the lists where I had pieces out, what I expected to come in, and wonder what I could possibly write about to bring in some money.*

As a travel writer I have always depended on externals. Let me alone in a place, especially one that has no past associations, and I can go to town. I need the excitement of the unfamiliar, of being on the move, in order to function. And I have always trusted the eye. But then there is something in a writer that is a *voyeur*. And there's nothing like a seaside resort to cater for it. Perhaps it was this that was responsible for my early attraction to Carnbray.

But the place has long since lost its curiosity for me. And since the money has run out and I'm stuck the way we are, here, I have been forced to write against the bias. (I have, in the past, always gone out to get my copy. I've never had to fall back on myself for material.) So these confessions. I began them out of desperation one morning in April with the rain coming down outside and the town grey and empty as the sea. Emily has asked: 'How come someone as intelligent as you has got himself into this position? Stuck in a cut-off seaside town. How come you let it happen?'

And I didn't know what to answer.

Emily stopped the part-time teaching because of an eye infection. That meant no lights in the room she was in, until the eye cleared up. I read to her from the newspapers until it was too dark and we went to bed.

Chapter Six

FROM TIME TO TIME editors have asked me for a short bio-graphical note about myself. I usually send them something like this. 'Joseph Grand. Born 1926, in Poland. Came to Canada when parents emigrated in 1929. Joined the R.C.A.F. in 1944. Flew over Europe from Air Force stations in England. After the war returned to England. Married an English girl. Travel writer.'

Of course I change the details depending on who is getting the biography. But what a lot is left out.

First of all I don't know when I was born. As a family we have never celebrated birthdays. I think mine was in September or October, I'm not sure. It's the business of having to live with two calendars. When I enlisted I decided to fix a date and keep it. I chose November 2nd. And for a while felt I was someone else like people who change names. But I don't pretend to myself. When I come across a horoscope in a magazine I look at both Scorpio and Libra. Then this place in Poland that's on my passport. Rakow. I don't remember a thing about it.

'We had a very nice house,' Mother said. 'And it was our property. I don't know what happened because we never sold it. It was beautiful. And we had a servant. When we were coming to Canada she wanted that I should take her with me. That's what I needed in this country.'

The samovar* in the dining-room on the dresser ... the large silver coins with two heads on one side and the double eagle on the other ...

'Why did you leave?'

'It's time you were asleep,' she said.

---

*Hearing Garachi Booblitchki – just the tune, no words – on TV last night. It was played slow. And it showed a doctor in some provincial Russian place waiting for the trains to start to run again. It was played slow and it sounded sad. When we had the record in Ottawa I used to turn the speed up so it went fast, Garachi Booblitchki ... it sounded very gay.

28

Years later I asked again.

'Because taxes were high,' she said. 'They would shoot at the peasants in the field.'

It's the only answer she gave me.

I say I don't remember anything of those first three years. But in 1953 we were living in London just off the Gloucester Road. There was a small Polish delicatessen by the Gloucester Road Tube Station (it is there no longer). Emily had sent me out to get a rye bread. But as soon as I got in I saw the candies. They had paper wrapping of a light brown cow. I asked the man behind the counter.

'Are these candies from Poland?'

'Yes,' he said.

I bought some and went out. I had forgotten about the bread. As soon as I closed the door I unwrapped a candy. The red neon from the Italian restaurant across the road flashed on and off in a rain puddle as the light fudge dissolved in the mouth. And the taste brought back a white house with green doors. Myself as a child looking out from a top window. It is autumn. A group of men are outside. One is smoking a cigar and wearing different clothes from the others. I ask mother about that man. 'He used to live here,' she said. 'Now he lives in America. He has come for a visit.'

We went to Ottawa because mother's uncle Saul was already there. In Poland, Saul painted designs on the ceilings of the large houses. In Ottawa he ran a wholesale banana business. This information was given to me the last time I was in Ottawa doing a travel piece and saw Saul's only son, Carleton, who runs the business. Carleton drove me to his house for dinner, in a new black Cadillac with black leather seats, and described the arrival of my father.

'We were allowed to stay up late. Our cousin from Europe was coming. My father expected someone quite young – after all your mother was in her early twenties. And someone who could do rough work. Instead there appeared this dandy in the Union Station with a silver-topped stick. He was small and bald and in his forties. We tried to get him interested in the banana business. But he couldn't or wouldn't learn the language. He would go to one of the workmen, point to a bunch of bananas and say *shnite*.'

I thought it ironic. Father's troubles began because he

couldn't learn English. And here am I trying to make my living from it.

'The best thing that could have happened to him,' Carleton said, 'was to have gone back to Poland. On the next boat.'

I thought of concentration camps, gas ovens.

I would lose the proportion of these confessions if I set down every step that took me from Ottawa to this decaying seaside town in the south of England.

I left school as soon as I could, went to work for 'Modern Goods', one of the cheap clothing stores in By Ward Market. Mr Mimico, the owner, taught me how to sell badly cut 'garments' (as he called them) to the farmers from the outskirts of Ottawa and the poor French from Lower Town. He was a short stout man with a paunch and a black moustache. For some reason he liked the letter M. His children were called Maynard and Mildred. And when we weren't busy he stood by the door watching the traffic.

'Meat Market – that's two more.' Or, 'Moses Bilsky just went by – that makes fifteen today.' He was on the lookout for signs, advertisements, anything that began with the letter M. Once he was trying to sell a French Canadian farmer a suit. They had gone outside to see how the cloth looked in the daylight. Suddenly Mr Mimico called out.

'*Medjuk.*'

The farmer looked startled.

'Where?' I said.

'On that green delivery truck going to Dalhousie Street.'

Businesses, like families, have a private language. And that was ours.

I was with Mr Mimico just over a year then went to Montreal and got a job with a small record company on St Catherine Street. The owner was an impressive Englishman called Bonati Harris. ('My father was in a boat called *Bonati* off Gallipoli. There was a torpedo coming towards them. All the others jumped off, he remained. He probably was too scared to jump. The thing was a dud. So I was called Bonati.') Harris believed that everyone would want a record of his or her voice. 'Just like people want a photograph.' I spent most of the time looking through the social pages of *The Star* and *The Gazette* to see who was getting married, confirmed, or had a bar-mitzvah. Then I'd get on the telephone to try and convince them they needed a record of the event. In the small studio I also interviewed commercial travellers, merchant seamen, tourists ... who bought copies of the interview to send to relatives and friends. It was meant to sound as if they were celebrities being interviewed on a Montreal radio programme.

I lived in two rooms above an undertaker on Sherbrooke East. When people discovered this several asked if I could arrange for them to see a corpse. Winterman, the undertaker, agreed. In no time this viewing snowballed. Until I was taking around parties of a dozen or more at fifty cents a head. (Winterman took twenty per cent.) Through Winterman I got to know the other undertakers in Montreal. Tours were laid on three nights a week. We'd go from one funeral parlour to another. When someone well-known died or if there had been a murder – I've had as many as five tours in a night.

At eighteen I joined the Air Force. It was 1944. The Air Force wanted evidence of a past. I didn't know mine. And the parts I did know I didn't like. So I began to change things. (People I grew up with were always changing their names.) I told Georgette, a French Canadian girl I was taking out, from St Hyacinthe, who worked as a typist in the same building as the record company, that my mother was French Canadian, father was Irish, and they were living in Quebec City. My next girl-friend, an older woman, a nurse in the Montreal General, was English. I told her my parents came from Hampshire and had retired in Vancouver. At the dance after the passing-out parade I was entrusted with escorting a debutante who seemed not at all interested until I told her I was illegitimate. When I went overseas I kept giving more variations on the biography. It all depended on who I was with. And when the war was over I came back to Montreal, saw that the government paid you to go to university. The registrar at McGill asked me what marks I had for junior matric. I gave myself average marks in everything except English and History. After that it was hard to take McGill seriously. I promoted myself from Pilot Officer to Flight Lieutenant. The Majors, the Captains, the Squadron Leaders, didn't mind. We were all undergraduates together.

'You don't look like a Jew,' one of the Majors said. He didn't like Jews. Neither did the others. Neither did I, but for different reasons. If I met any Jews on the campus who stuck together and went to the Hillel club, I had nothing to do with them. Yet on my own I'd sneak over to Waxman's restaurant on Park Avenue. When I stayed with the Dean of Christ Church Cathedral, rented his large basement room, (you couldn't get more c. of e. in Montreal than that) I'd go off on my own to Waxman's for gefilte fish, helzel, lutkas, and to watch the others eat. Even now when I go to London one of the first things I do is go to Blooms for a meal. I thought I put the Jewish business behind me by marrying an English girl. Just as I thought I could forget about Canada by going over to live in England. But that is going ahead.

In my final year at McGill I wrote the words to the song *Lilac Lou*. This by itself is not important except the other side of the record had a song that became very popular in 1949. I received five thousand dollars as my share of the royalties. And with this I joined the Captains, the Majors, the Squadron Leaders, who were going back to England on private incomes. Nostalgia because of the war. Perhaps? I liked wartime England. The territory was wide open. And coming back was also pleasant. The Captains, the Majors, had connections.* Their families in Canada knew families in England. I was taken to weekend do's in country houses. The bust by Epstein by the stairs in the hall. The lengthy meals with many courses and wines and the mothers complaining that England was dull, that their daughters were not having the times they had. The eightsome reels, the Hunt Balls, nothing to drink but champagne while the orchestra played the Harry Lime theme.

Then postwar England began to assert itself. The queues, the cold houses falling into decay, the war damage, the cube of butter once a week, the ten cigarettes under the counter. What I didn't realize was just how much this seediness appealed. The Majors and the Captains didn't like it. In the spring they left for Paris, the South of France, Tangier. I went with some others to Carnbray.

Carnbray was a very different place in 1949. The tourists hadn't found it. The rich had. I remember seeing men and

---

At that time I still regarded my future seriously. I was still ambitious.

women in evening dress walking along the uncrowded front in the light summer evenings. I probably became a travel writer because of that first summer. I had come straight from city life in Montreal. And to be exposed, unexpectedly, to so much varied nature gave me an exhilarating sense of personal freedom. I spent most of the time outside just walking and looking. For much of what I was seeing I was totally ignorant. The names of the birds (apart from plain gull and sparrow) I didn't know. I didn't know the names of the flowers or what was gorse or bracken or heather or blackberries or these stunted English trees. The fish I saw up for auction every morning at the slipway with their fat human lips and small eyes were anonymous. A hard and new physical world seemed to have suddenly opened before me, and in such splendid colour. I'd get up before six in the morning and go out. And late at night I'd be sitting by the window, just so I wouldn't miss anything.

I met Emily at the end of the summer just as the money from *Lilac Lou* was coming to an end. She was on the beach lying on the sand, getting a tan, and reading a book. I was with some rich Canadians I knew from McGill who were doing Europe and reading Scott Fitzgerald. Next week they were going to Italy. One was saying, 'You should see *The Lady's Not for Burning.* Christopher Fry's a lot better than T.S. Eliot.' Another said: 'Did I tell you I had tea with a Lord?'

'I'll only be a minute,' I said.

'Where are you going?'

'I'm going to ask that girl if she'll come and have tea with us.'

I walked over the fine shell sand to where Emily was.

'Would you like to have tea?'

She looked very attractive, nice cheekbones, a small nose, a small mouth, light eyes, blonde short hair. She was reading *The Gentleman from San Francisco.*

'Are those your friends?'

'Yes,' I said.

'No thank you.' She went back to her book.

I walked back to the Canadians.

'She doesn't want to,' I said.

We watched and listened to the surf breaking, the swimmers coming in on it, the small children jumping in the shallows. Then the Canadians said it was time to go to the hotel.

'I'll join you later,' I said.

When they had gone off the beach I walked back to Emily.

'We can have tea by ourselves.'

We went and had Cornish cream with some rolls and jam in The Balmoral, a small café facing the sea in the least crowded part of the front. We sat by a window, watched the French Crabbers with their mizzens up anchored in the bay. She told me her name, that she was on holiday staying on a farm, near Carnbray, where she had been evacuated during the war.

I told her that I was an ex-Flight Lieutenant, that my father was in wood, that we had two houses in Ottawa, one by a lake.

Only later was I to know that I didn't have to, that I could have played it straight with her all along.

Chapter Seven

*Story I wrote about the first five years of our married life
when we lived in a series of places in and around London.*

GORDON RIDEAU'S eyes were closed and he could hear the
trucks going by outside the window on the main London to
Guildford road. And in between the trucks the alarm clock on
the floor. At his feet the hot water bottle was cold. He shoved
it to the edge of the bed. Then he opened his eyes and saw the
wallpaper: wide yellow bars separated by thin black lines.

His wife, Coral, lay with several blankets over her so that
just her dark hair was sticking out. Between them a National
Health orange bottle was wrapped in a nappie to keep the milk
inside it warm in case the baby woke during the night.

He could hear Kate walking down the stairs. The hall light
was on. The brown curtains across the bedroom were drawn.
The room was cold. There was a pitcher standing in a large
basin, both had a red rose painted on the enamel. And a large
bedpan with an old copy of *Vogue* on top. A small triptych of
three angels stood on the mantel above the small fireplace
which was stuffed with newspapers, cardboard, and bits of
coloured crêpe paper. All this they had inherited from the
owner. Their belongings: a steel trunk was open in a corner, in
another corner two smaller trunks. Inside were clothes
jumbled and spilling out.

Coral sat up quickly, turned back the cover, and looked
closely down one leg. Near the ankle she picked off a flea and,
carefully, crushed it between her fingers. Then she left the
bed.

Gordon watched her. There is nothing graceful about her
movements, he thought. She was wearing a grey sweater and
put on a blue shirt. She took the nappie with the make-shift
milk bottle, the alarm clock, and went downstairs.

Now he lay in bed in a sense of luxury. He was alone, staying in. He drew his knees up to keep warm. He heard the radio
downstairs playing dance music. And lay there wondering

whether she would bring him a cup of tea.

A door opened below and Kate called out.

'Breakfast is ready Daddy.'

'Coming,' he said.

And remained in bed knowing that in a few minutes she would open the door again and say:

'Breakfast is ready Daddy.'

And he would say:

'I'm just getting my socks on.'

But he had them on all night, and his shirt, and a heavy black sweater.

The child came lightly up the stairs. She had just turned four. A shy attractive child with blonde straight hair and fine small features.

'OK,' Gordon said as she came into the bedroom. 'I'm coming.'

'Post, Daddy.'

She gave him a brown envelope.

He opened it. It was a letter from the electricity company saying that a man had come yesterday to disconnect the electricity but no one was in. He was going to come on Friday at eleven unless they could pay £12 5 2d.

It means a trip to London, Gordon thought. And that was enough to make him get up.

He dressed and went to the window and pulled back the brown curtain. The diagonal crack in the glass was like a scar. The fields, across the road, muddy and drab. The trees on the border of the field – misshapen by the ivy that was slowly killing them – looked very pretty. He watched a motorcycle accelerate as it went by splashing mud on either side and with a muddy wake. Then he closed the light in their bedroom and went down a narrow passage. By the children's open door: the smell of urine, the camp bed, the mug of water, the comics and books on top of an overturned orange case. He turned sharply. Down the narrow stairs. At the bottom he opened a door and immediately felt the warm air. It was the one room that was warm. A coal fire was going in the fireplace. Beside it, in a corner, was a baby's cot.

Kate stood by the cot dressed in a jumper, a red sweater, which someone had given them when their own children had grown out of the clothes. She was talking to the baby. 'Ah goolie goo Rachel. Ah goolie goo.' The baby stood up in the cot grasping the wooden struts and gurgled back a couple of vowels. She looked like something caught in a cage.

'Good morning,' Gordon said cheerfully to the children and went into the kitchen.

Coral was at the stove. 'High keeps changing,' she said. 'I don't know if the hot plate is off or on.'

'Use the Master Switch.'

Then he decided it would be better to show her. 'Off' he said and put the switch up. 'On' he pulled it down.

'What do you want,' she said. 'There's a bit of cheese – I could make toast.'

'Fine,' he said and went into the other room. Kate was playing with some pieces of paper and a pencil. The baby was crawling on the floor to the coal bucket. She took pieces of coal and tried to put them in her mouth. Her lips were black. Gordon took the bucket away and put it behind a chair. The child crawled after it.

'What post did you have?' she said bringing in the toast and cheese.

'A reminder from the electricity.'

'When are they coming?'

'Tomorrow.' He tried to appear casual. 'I guess I'll have to go to London.'

'Where Daddy going?' Kate said quickly.

'To London – I'll bring you back something.'

'A dolly,' the child said excitedly.

'What will you do,' Coral said.

'I'll try the bank first – I'll find a way.'

'You know how I hate this place.'

'I know.'

And he prepared himself for her to follow with: you can always get away but I'm stuck here ... my hands are tied ... I'm the one that's always left behind. Instead, she said: 'When you're up could you look around.'

'I'll go and see some real estate people.'

'Try somewhere near a park.'

'I'll try darling.'

'This isn't just you saying things to keep me happy? You will do something.'

'Yes,' he said quietly.

'We've got less than two months.'

'You know how I work.' He tried to sound convincing. 'Leave things until the last week. Then I get something.'

She didn't reply. He was nearly there, he thought.

'You won't forget.'

And he was safe now.

'I'll do my best darling,' he said and got up. 'I'd better shave.'

There was some hot water left in the kettle. He emptied it in a tin mould that she used to make cakes in, mixed a bit of cold water from the tap, and shaved in front of the mirror, above the dishes.

He tried to tidy his sideburns and realized that his face looked odd. It was the eyes. The left one set at an angle. He saw it as well in the baby. Around the small mirror was the kitchen window with old spider webs. Cuts in the snow skiers make climbing a hill sideways. And for a moment he was back to the pressure the cold made on his forehead. He was in a sleigh sitting behind the swaying rump of a horse held in its tight harness, with Holly. Past white fields with the telegraph poles just protruding. I could tell, she said, when you held my hand to take my coat off. And Jasmine. It snowed all that day in Montreal. After the lecture we went to the Berkeley and drank brandy alexanders until it was time to go. The expensive gloom of her parents' apartment. The thing like a curled bulrush that she took out from her hair. And Lily. How quick it was with her ... she had her own car. Her father owned an entire small town in Northern Ontario. He wondered what would have happened to his life had he made one of them pregnant.

'Don't forget to empty the bucket,' Coral called from the other room.

He took the spade from the shed, walked along the path to the back garden. Half way down he selected a part of bare earth and began to dig. He emptied the almost full black bucket into the hole he made. Then shovelled the earth back into the hole. It splashed gently. Then the liquid overflowed and stained the earth. He came back into the kitchen. 'I've emptied the bucket,' he said to Coral. He washed his hands. 'Is there anything left?'

She went to the dresser with the few dishes and from a Peter Rabbit saucer took out a halfpenny and a threepenny stamp. He put the halfpenny in his pocket. Then went upstairs, into his room, and put on his one clean white shirt. He took down his trousers hanging from a hook on a hanger in the corner. They were the trousers of his one remaining suit. He saw how frayed the bottoms were. He took the small scissors from his desk and cut some of the hanging threads. He put on the trousers, his tie and jacket. And came down carrying the black winter overcoat that he bought ten years ago when he was at university. He put it on. Coral brushed him down. The children were crowding around him.

'You look nice Daddy,' Kate said.

'You will look around,' Coral said.

'Yes,' he said, then smiled to the children.

'I'll bring you back something nice.'

'A dolly?' Kate said.

'Something to eat.'

Coral picked up the baby.

He kissed them all goodbye.

They went with him to the front gate. And watched him walk along the road away from them. Kate climbed up the wooden gate and said goodbye several times. And they waved to each other.

From a distance of ten yards, Coral thought, he was still handsome and looked neat and successful. There was the confident manner, the upright walk. He turned and waved back to them. From some thirty yards, she thought, he looked even better. He might have been an executive going off to the office, to work.

He looked for darkness in the windshield. He could tell quickly by the amount of darkness, the outline (like those outlines they had trained him to look at in a tenth, a twentieth, a fiftieth of a second) whether the driver of the coming car was alone or not. He didn't bother to put up his hand if there were two.

From Piccadilly Gordon walked down Lower Regent Street and into the bank, across the light marble floor, to the short teller with the Italian sounding name. They shook hands. And asked each other questions as if they knew one another well.

'I've just come up for the day,' Gordon said.

'How is the family?'

'Fine. And yours?'

'They're fine. We went to Connemara for a holiday.' He smiled and took out some photographs. 'It was wonderful – the best holiday we had.'

There were photographs of some children by a pony, by a cottage. And the bank teller in a pair of shorts.

'May I see the manager?'

'I'll see if he is free.'

He left his cage and out of it looked even smaller but long in the arms.

He came back smiling. 'The manager is busy. But our assistant manager Mr Henderson will see you.'

'Come in Mr Rideau.'

The assistant manager, unlike most North Americans, looked much older than his forty-two years. But his 'Sit down Mr Rideau. Cigarette?' had a professional warmth. 'Now, what's the trouble?'

'I have an electricity bill just over twelve pounds that I must meet tomorrow or else they'll cut us off. Could the bank let me overdraw fifteen pounds? It will only be for a short time. I've got money coming in.'

'I'm sorry. It's impossible.' The assistant manager said. 'I can't let you have a pound.' He lowered his voice. '*He* gave me strict instructions.' And his eyes indicated the frosted glass partition of the other room.

'But I've been with the bank for seven years.'

'He doesn't consider you a banking proposition.'

They were both silent. The assistant manager looked uncomfortable. 'Are you a veteran?'

'Yes,' Gordon said. 'I was in the Army.' And remembered a time in Montreal, after taking a girl home to the Town of Mount Royal he flagged a cab and found he didn't have enough money to get back. He told this to the driver. 'Are you a veteran,' the driver asked.

'I was in the Air Force,' the assistant manager said. He crushed his cigarette in the green-glass ashtray. Then stood up and walked away from his desk. Gordon also got up. The assistant manager put his hands in his trouser pockets.

'I'm sorry I can't let you have the money. Take this. Pay it back when you can. Please.'

'Thanks. I'll pay it back soon as I can.'

'There's no rush.'

He wondered if the assistant manager was now going to give him a lecture. But they shook hands and said goodbye.

Outside, walking up the Haymarket, Gordon took the bill out and saw it was a five pound note. He was delighted. Imagine getting money from an assistant bank manager I had never met. But a moment later it also registered on him that the probable reason he got the money was because the assistant manager had never laid eyes on him before.

At a small kiosk he bought a pack of tipped Gauloises, a box of matches, an *Evening Standard.* Then walked along Piccadilly to Lyons Corner House. He went into the Wimpy side, found an empty table by the wall, ordered two hamburgers and a black coffee. Around the centre counter North Americans were staring at other North Americans. It might have been the drugstore back home, except they were on good behaviour.

The alarm clock woke Mr and Mrs Black at seven though Mr Black wasn't going to work. He went to shave. And used the foam lather of the company whose assistant accountant he was. Then he sat down in the room with the Van Gogh print on the wall, the souvenir ashtray from Clovelly, the silver napkin rings, the photograph of himself in the Home Guard, while Mrs Black did his porridge and two pieces of toast in the kitchen.

'You won't get excited,' Mrs Black said as they were having their second cup of tea.

'No dear.'

'She could have her old room. The children could sleep in the spare room. And there's the camp bed.'

Mr Black put on the jacket of his dark suit, the homburg hat, the black coat. He was a handsome if stern looking man with dark straight hair, a lean face, but there was a strain about it, the result of a lifetime of bronchial trouble.

'Do you want to take anything for the train?' Mrs Black said, standing by the glass enclosed cabinet with her Mary Webb novels and his *Lord Jim,* James Agate, *Quest for Corvo,* the books on accountancy.

'I have the paper.'

'I hope it goes all right,' Mrs Black said at the door.

'I'll be back for tea. Goodbye dear.'

The train went by Eltham, Kidbrooke, Lewisham. Mr Black turned to the *Telegraph's* crossword: -------- is mortals' chiefest enemy' (Shakespeare). He tried 'dying'. But that wasn't long enough. Neither was 'boredom'. 'Temptation' was too long.

At Charing Cross he changed to a tube that took him to Victoria and here he had to wait another ten minutes for a train to Horsham. At Horsham he took a taxi to the cottage. It was 10:20 when he opened the front gate but he didn't go to the front door. He went around the side of the cottage where he surprised Coral hanging up the children's washing.

'Hullo,' he said quietly.

They smiled then they kissed. And one could see a family resemblance.

She opened the kitchen door and led him into the warm room where he took off his coat.

'How is Mummy?'

'She sends her love.'

He gave the children some toffee candy.

'Gordon is in London,' she said. 'He had to go up on business.'

'Daddy is going to bring me a dolly,' Kate said.

'We haven't had our milk,' Coral said. 'I could make tea without it.'

Mr Black sat in the worn red chair. His breathing was audible. 'You can't go on like this,' he said quietly.

Coral quickly took the children into the next room and closed the door behind them.

'Why don't you leave him,' Mr Black said. 'I'll see that you and the children are looked after. I'll get you a house —'

She didn't reply.

'He's no good,' he said. 'He'll only drag you down.'

'I can't leave him,' she said.

'If he wants to go on like this there's no reason why you and the children —'

'He's got no one except me and the children.'

'I'll get you a house —' He began, but he knew it had not gone right. This wasn't the way he had rehearsed it.

'I think you must hate me,' Coral said.

'I don't hate you,' Mr Black said. But he was at a loss as to what to say next.

Kate came into the room followed by the crawling baby. Kate had a drawing. 'This is for you Grandpa.' He took the drawing and gave the child a half-crown. He also gave Coral three one-pound notes. She immediately went next door to the grocery and came back with milk, sugar, and some biscuits. They sat in the warm room and had tea while Mr Black told her about a cousin who had gone to Rhodesia to run an Outward Bound school. That an uncle had become manager of a bank in Plymouth. And another cousin had gone to Canada as a physical training instructor. It was time, he said, he was leaving. They walked slowly up the road to the Shell garage where Mr Black took a taxi. Kate kissed him. So did Coral.

'Goodbye Daddy,' she said.

* * *

For half an hour Gordon sat in the cubicle by the wall of the Wimpy watching other people. Then he went downstairs to the washroom. He turned the hot tap of the sink and began to wash his hands.

'You can always tell a McGill man. He washes his hands *before* —'

Gordon turned to see a grinning boyish face. I don't know him, he thought. Aloud he said. 'Of course. It's —'

'Not fair surprising you like this. I'm Hugh Finlay,' the man said still grinning.

'Hugh Finlay,' Gordon said. They shook hands. 'What are you doing here?'

'Passing through. I'm on the way south, to France.'

They were both in their early thirties, McGill graduates, in London, but there the resemblance stopped abruptly. Hugh Finlay was blond, ruddy, and radiated bodily comfort.

'I heard you were over here,' Finlay said. 'I was going to go to the bank to get your address. You know we're having a reunion?'

'No.' Gordon said. 'No, I didn't.'

'It's our tenth anniversary.'

They returned to the cubicle and ordered two coffees.

'You've worn well, Hugh.' Gordon said.

'The reward for leading a healthy life,' Finlay said. 'You married?'

'Yes. We've got two kids.'

'Do I know her?'

'No. She's an English girl. We live in the country. How about you?'

'I was engaged to Sally Boston. The Boston Biscuits. They give a quarter of a million each year *anonymously*. But she was too good. She's like an angel. If she saw somebody poor, she'd cry.' He took some coloured snapshots from his jacket pocket. 'This is my yacht at Cannes. Here's a picture of Garbo on it. Here's some of the girls I had on board last summer. She's only sixteen. Hard to believe. Do you know any addresses of girls?'

The pretty West Indian waitress came with the two cups of coffee. Gordon insisted on paying.

'How about coming to the reunion?' Hugh said suddenly. 'Lots of the gang you know will be there.'

'Do you think it will be all right?'

'I know it will. I'll phone Charlie Bishop.'

While he was gone Gordon tried to remember Hugh Finlay at McGill ... but he couldn't.

'I talked to Charlie. He said sure, swell. We've a couple of hours. How about if we get some fresh air. I've a rented car outside.'

They were driving through Hyde Park when Hugh Finlay said. 'I saw a friend of yours last week. Mary Savage. Except she's not Mary Savage any more she's Mary Troy. Remember Jack? You'll see him at the reunion.'

'How is Mary.'

'Exactly the same. She does some kind of social work.'

'What's Jack doing?'

'Selling beans ... millions of them. They've got a place by the river. Fifteen rooms but no kids. I think they're planning to adopt one.'

Because her father left her the money Coral decided to go into London with the children. She washed them and herself, got them dressed, caught a green bus to the station then a train to Victoria.

From Victoria she took a bus to Kensington Gardens. And walked through the Gardens. A man was flying a kite, ducks flew over. The children chased the wood pigeons. She liked London. It was the only place she wanted to live. But what chance had they? She decided to try the Town Hall. The receptionist led her into a separate office where a single yellow rose in a thin glass vase stood on the wooden desk. 'Mrs Troy will be here in a minute.'

A tall angular woman with dark hair and glasses came in. The woman was about the same age as Coral, perhaps a year or two older. 'What's the problem,' she said.

'We have to get out of the place we're living in ... in Sussex ... and I wonder if you can help us find somewhere in London?'

'You have no alternative accommodation?'

'No.'

'Have you funds?'

'No. We haven't.'

'Does your husband live with you?'

'Yes.'

'I'm sorry. I'm afraid I can't help you. We can only help if your husband leaves you.'

Coral came out with the children and walked along Kensington High Street. Everyone it seemed would help her if he left her, or if she left him. Otherwise, what was the future? Moving from one rented place to another, from country village to country village or, with luck, to a provincial town. And she hated living in other people's houses.

She caught a bus to Trafalgar Square and walked among the pigeons. The children clung to her. Then along the Mall. She bought some choc-ices and they had a little picnic of choc-ices on a bench in St James's Park. She wondered where Gordon was, who he was seeing, what he was doing. He always came back with money and food from these trips to London. But she suspected that he never told her the whole truth as to how he got it.

She was walking through the Park – the baby in the pushchair, Kate holding her hand – when a truck, with a camera on the roof, stopped. A man and woman were inside. The man said. 'Do you mind being in a film? Just like you are ... with your children. Can you do that again? Thank you. Thank you very much.' A few minutes later, further into the Park, she sat on the grass, underneath a beech, by the water. The sun was out. Kate was feeding the ducks, the baby was on the grass watching. She suddenly felt extraordinarily happy. She hoped the truck would come back and take a picture of them now.

45

Well-dressed men in their middle to late thirties were standing under the hanging flags or by the windows looking out to Trafalgar Square. They greeted one another enthusiastically. They came up to Gordon Rideau.

'Hi, Gordy old man.'

'Where have you been hiding?'

'Hello Gordon,' Charlie Bishop said and shook hands. 'Nice of you to come. It has been a long time.'

'Ten years.'

'You don't look any different Gordon.'

Mike Gagnon an energetic head of a publishing firm who was tipped while an undergraduate to be the next Prime Minister came up. 'Let's in on the secret Gordy. How do you keep slim? You wearing a corset?' Mike's fine features were slowly being undermined by fat. 'I go to the Y three times a week but I've still got this rubber ring.' And he playfully slapped his middle.

Charlie Bishop hit his glass with a spoon and called Quiet. Quiet. A short stocky man with glasses, almost bald, but hardly a line in his face. He was a director in the London branch of his grandfather's tar company.

'As you know,' he said confidently, 'this is something of an occasion. Our tenth anniversary. And while the main one is being celebrated in Montreal it is fitting that we in London should get together and remember when we all were ...'

'Single,' someone shouted.

'*And* broke,' another replied.

He waited. 'The bond we established at McGill was something special. It's a different kind of loyalty to anything else. It's different from the wife or the kids. And I know that every time we come and get together like this that bond is strengthened.'

'Hear, hear,' came from several tables.

'This year I have a surprise. And by now you all must know who the surprise is. He's sitting here beside me ... Somebody has pointed out that our year was a vintage year. And it's true. We've got more people in the Canadian edition of *Time* than any year since. But the only literary man we produced was Gordy. He has lived in England, in the country, since he left us. And he is difficult to get hold of. But when I heard he would be in London today I didn't have to do much persuading to get him to come to this reunion. Fellow classmates, I'm very proud to give you Gordon Rideau.'

There was generous applause. Gordon got up.

'I first would like to say how pleased I am to be back with you.'

'Hey, where did you pick up that Limey accent?' Jack Troy called out. Charlie Bishop detected something else in Gordon's voice and wondered why he was so nervous.

'Although this is the first reunion that I have attended. I've often thought of my college days,' he said hesitantly. 'I really had a good time. And I was just old enough to know it ... I think what made us different from the other years was because we were all returning veterans. And it was difficult to pretend we were college kids straight from high school ...'

He's not a good speaker, thought Charlie Bishop. His voice is too monotonous. But he seems to have the right idea. It looks like a short speech.

'... and that nice secure feeling of walking under the avenue of black trees in winter or in the fall sitting on the grass under the willow ...'

Hugh Finlay seemed, at that moment, to be sitting on the grass under the willow tree watching the grey squirrels, the fallen leaves, on the lawns; and waiting for a two o'clock lecture.

'One is always disappointed by change,' Gordon said coming to the end. 'And these reunions remain a tribute. To one's youth. To gaiety. To optimism. When things seemed continually fresh. And life was a pleasure. And it was all so very easy.'

He sat down quickly to loud applause. Charlie Bishop leaned over and shook Gordon's hand. So did Mike Gagnon from the other side.

Then Charlie Bishop got up, thanked Gordon for his speech. 'Before we leave the formal side,' Charlie said, 'I'd like us all to stand and remember those classmates who are not here with us.'

They got up, some bowed their heads slightly. Charlie waited then nodded to Jack Troy. And Jack began to sing. Holding hands the rest joined in. There were tears in Hugh Finlay's eyes as, with the others, he sang.

For auld lang syne, my dear,

For auld lang syne,
We'll tak' a cup o' kindness yet
For the days of auld lang syne!

They broke up into small groups around separate tables. And as the afternoon went on, the food, the drink, being guest of honour did something to Gordon Rideau. He went around gaily from one group to another. And he found himself boasting about things that hadn't happened.

'The Russians have brought out my last two novels,' he said, cutting into one group's conversation. 'But I can't spend those roubles unless I go there.'

To another. 'They're making a film in Ireland. It's called *The Millionaire*. I did the script. It's an original.'

A few moments later he tried again. 'I won some prize in Australia. But I don't believe it. How can you believe a telegram that's signed Johnny Soprano?'

But after a while of this he felt their lack of interest. And that he was being left out of the conversation. The others were talking away and they wouldn't let him come in. He had the feeling that he was no longer wanted.

If anyone was watching this convivial gathering he would have seen, through the smoke of cigarettes and cigars, Mike Gagnon get up from the table shortly after five and make his way across the room to the toilet. Gordon Rideau got up and followed him. They were in there a few minutes. Then they came out together, not talking. Some ten minutes later, Charlie Bishop made his way to the toilet. And Gordon left his chair soon after Charlie disappeared. They came out together, Charlie somewhat red in the face.

In the next half-hour Gordon followed three more into the toilet and reappeared with each one.

The talk around the table where Gordon Rideau sat was noticeably subdued. A short while later he got up and said he had to go. 'It's a great reunion,' he said to Charlie Bishop. He wanted to shake Charlie's hand, but Charlie withdrew his. 'See you ...'

After he had gone, Charlie Bishop, Mike Gagnon, Jack Troy, Hugh Finlay, sat around without saying anything. They looked tired.

'Our great author,' Mike Gagnon said finally.

'Maybe he's had a run of hard luck,' Jack Troy said.

48

'How much did he hit you?'

'Three pounds.'

'He got that from me.'

'That four-flusher —' Hugh said, his voice shaking.

'You guys got off easy,' Charlie Bishop said. 'He hit me for five.'

'That little four-flusher.' Suddenly Hugh lashed out at a glass on the table. Then he saw it was on the floor in pieces.

'Don't take it so hard,' Charlie Bishop said. 'There's another one next year. I won't make the same mistake.'

'But why ...?' Hugh said. 'Why did he spoil everything?'

Chapter Eight

ALTHOUGH I'm doing confessions, I feel I'm still thinking as a travel writer. Am I not using 'being hard-up' (it's my main excitement) the way I used travelling before? I tell myself, I have to go deeper. But am I going deeper? Or am I just behaving like a travel writer and, instead of a landscape, skimming over Emily's life and mine. Are things 'deeper' just because you go into yourself? Perhaps a writer wasn't what I was cut out for at all. I feel I was meant to be on the move. As soon as I start to travel, then the writing starts. It's almost a compulsion. And now we're stuck in this seaside town.

Emily said it was a mistake to come back. And perhaps she was right. But at the time we hadn't much choice. We had to get out of Sussex and we had no money. The only place I knew where it was possible to rent something cheap, as it was out of season, was Carnbray.

I had been away from Carnbray six years. And in that time the necessity of writing to earn a living forced a discipline on me. When we came back Carnbray felt marvellous at first. There was no atmosphere of work about the place. I walked down to the harbour. A warm sunny day. Looked at the ribbed sand, the water in the bay, the far shore fields, the gulls. Walked over to one of the beaches. The blue, the green, canvas windbreakers were up in the sand. When the sun caught them they glistened like pieces of coloured glass. How it brought back that first summer. The place hadn't changed. It seemed that I had. Alone, I was corruptible. I could have moved on with the Captains, the Majors, the Squadron Leaders. To the South of France, Tangier, or even back to Montreal. But Emily (always telling the truth), the children, the need to earn some money, was like a conscience. I began to hate this place and what it represented.

'Why don't you go out?' Emily said. 'Do you know it's over a week that you haven't been out of the house.'

'I went out on Tuesday to the post office.'

'I meet people in the street. They all ask. And how is Joseph? What can I say? He's working. He's up in his room.

He's busy. Why don't you go out and see people?'

'It costs money to see people,' I said. 'If I meet anyone they say let's go in for a drink. I'm too old to go bumming.'

'So what do we do? Play cards, read newspapers, and watch television. I'm tired watching television.'

'You're tired when we go to bed.'

'You expect me to be excited just because we're going to bed? Why don't you go out for a walk now. You'll feel better. Walk around the harbour, or through the town, go to the library.'

'I hate this place,' I said. 'All I can think of is how to get us out. I've got a sign up on the wall of my room, *You've got to get out of here,* facing me all the time. I don't want to end my life in this cut-off seaside joint.'

The phone rang.

'You answer it.'

'Now you don't even want to answer the phone,' she said and went out of the room to the kitchen.

I went up to this room, looked at the collection of picture postcards stuck on the large mirror. (When I look in the mirror, to see myself, the postcards give a 3-D effect.) They were from people scattered over North America, Africa, Europe, or cards Albert sends when he goes away on holiday. I've stuck them on with sellotape with spaces of glass in between. I even have a postcard of Carnbray in with the others. A summer's day ... palm trees ... the sea a shade darker blue than the sky ... a large green and white yacht in the harbour ... people on a sand beach ...

As a postcard, I thought, I could like this place.

I went to my desk and looked at the pieces of paper listing what payments I expected to come in. They added up to £325. But I had learned not to count too much on other people paying when they said they would.

Next morning Emily had a letter from her mother in London, and with it came a money order for ten pounds for Christmas.

I got a small tree and put it up in the front room. I went and got some ivy and Emily put it around the room, on the walls near the ceiling. Cards began to come in. And I went out and had a drink in a pub with Jimmy and with other people I hadn't seen for several months.

On the evening of December 23rd we were waiting in the front room, which looked very nice and warm. We had a fire going in the fireplace. There were some coloured balls hanging from the lights. There was this nice fitting red carpet. It's a splendid room with a large bay window and we only use it when people come, or perhaps in summer, for it's too cold. Emily had made some sandwiches and I got a bottle of sherry and wrapped it in coloured paper, and bought some extra glasses. We were waiting for the people Emily had been evacuated to during the war. They lived near Truro. Since our marriage they've sent a chicken for Christmas and I've given them a bottle of sherry. We sat in the large second-hand chairs with the scratched sides where the cat sharpened its claws, waiting for them to come. It was past seven. I thought they were late.

'They have to put the cows away,' Emily said, 'and do a lot of things before they can leave.'

A few minutes later we heard sounds outside the front door.

'That's them.'

'No,' I said, without knowing why. And it wasn't.

It was a wizened, hunched-up little woman, determined, thrusting her face forward. It was not a pretty face, although it had new blondish curls.

'Does Joseph Grand live here?'

It wasn't so much a question as an assertion. And it was said by my sister Mona from Meridian. I hadn't seen her for ten years. Afterwards, she said I just stood there not saying anything but shaking my head.

I went outside and saw Oscar. He looked like a gentle wrestler. A squat little man with sleepy eyes. A hat on, a camera around his neck, a brand-new black coat and black gloves.

I shook Oscar's hand.

'Why didn't you write or phone or send a telegram?'

'I wanted to,' Oscar said. 'But your sister didn't let me.'

I looked into the taxi, half-expected to see my father and mother inside.

'I bet you're surprised,' Mona said excitedly when we got inside with the bags and hung up their coats. Oscar kept his hat on.

'Why didn't you let me know when you got to London?'

'We didn't want you to go to any trouble,' Mona said.

Oscar said: 'I've got a movie-camera – I wanted to record the expression on your face when you saw your sister.'

I steered them into the front room. Mona lit a cigarette.

'You don't look like your pictures, Emily,' Mona said. 'You've lost weight,' she said to me. 'It suits you. The last time I saw you, you were fat. I thought you had heart trouble.'

Then the kids were introduced.

'This is Martha – this is Ella – this is Rebecca —'

'They're like dolls,' Mona said.

'– this is your Uncle Oscar and your Auntie Mona. They've come all the way from Meridian in Canada. How was the trip?'

'Terrible,' Oscar said. 'We had to change twice on the train. You know it took longer to come down here from London than fly from Montreal over to England. Why do you live so far away?'

'If you sent a telegram or phoned,' I said, 'I would have told you what train to get – You wouldn't have had to change —'

'I told her,' Oscar said.

'I didn't want to put you to any trouble — Shall we give them the presents?'

They brought their new bags into the front room and brought out gay bunny pyjamas for the kids. They gave Emily a Norwegian ski sweater.

'He always wears black,' Mona said. 'Why, I don't know. So I thought I'd get him a white sweater.'

It was a splendid sweater with a turtle-neck.

'You smoke?' Oscar said. And gave me several red and white flat tins of duty-free cigarettes.

'Thanks. Why didn't you write from Canada?'

'We didn't know if we were coming or not. You know your sister. She was terrified of flying.'

'Everyone told us to go to Miami,' Mona said. 'At this time of the year England, they said, would be full of smog, fog, accidents.'

'It was a toss-up,' Oscar said, 'whether to go to Disneyland or to come here.'

'Didn't you know *some*thing was in the air when I didn't write?' Mona said.

I didn't say anything to that. I couldn't remember when she last wrote.

'Here,' Oscar said to the children, taking out his wallet

from his back buttoned-down pocket. 'From your Grannie and Grandpa in Canada – your Chanukah gelt.' And he gave them two pounds each. Our kids never had so much money.

My sister looked at the Christmas tree, the decorations, the cards.

'Do they know about Chanukah?'

The kids were silent.

'Your Daddy will tell you.' Then back to me in the same low disapproving voice.

'You celebrate Christmas?'

'We sort of have a tree – and I give out the presents on Christmas Day.'

'I always say, how you want to live your life that is your business,' Mona said.

The kids went upstairs to their rooms to try on their pyjamas.

'What would you like to drink?' I said confidently. It was the first time that year I had so much drink in the house. 'Scotch, gin, sherry, beer —'

'You have no rye?' Mona asked.

'No.'

'I won't bother.'

'Oscar. What'll you have?'

'I don't care for the stuff.'

'Won't anyone join me in a drink?'

'I'll have some sherry,' Emily said.

'Let me taste,' my sister said. 'It's not bad. I'll have a drop.'

'How's Maw and Paw?' I said.

'The same,' she said. 'Maw still works at the hospital.' Then suddenly brightening up. 'If they could only see the kids – Paw's got to go in for a check-up when we get back. You should see how nervous he was when we told him we were flying.'

I remember the last time I saw him. We were waiting for the taxi to take me to the station. He was in his shirt. A towel around his head. He was in the middle of shaving. 'I hope I'll still be here next time you come,' he said and began to weep. 'Sure Pop,' I said. How pathetic and kind he looked. Then we saw each other in the hall mirror. He pointed to his weeping face in the glass. 'I look like a Chinaman.'

I suggested to Emily that Mona and Oscar might like to have some coffee.

Mona hunted in one of their bags and came out with a jar of instant coffee, and gave it to Emily.

'We drink a lot of coffee, and I heard you can't get good coffee over here.'

'We've got instant coffee,' Emily said.

'Oh, you have,' Mona said, puzzled. 'Well, we like it strong.'

As soon as Emily was out of the room my sister said.

'I thought you said she was *half*-Jewish.'

'I said that long ago, because of Maw. She asked me where did I get married? Who was the rabbi? Now she knows. I know she knows. She said if this happened in her time the family would be sitting Shiva.'

'I always say, the way you live your life that's your business,' Mona said.

Emily came back with the coffee, and she also had some hamburgers in buns that she made earlier and heated up.

'Gee, these taste good,' Oscar said.

'They're like we make them,' Mona said, somewhat surprised.

I was surprised how she had aged. I knew she was two years younger. But she looked in her forties. Except for the body, which was very slim. She sat hunched, her back curved, jaw thrust forward, smoking one cigarette after another.

I heard a car go up. We live on the side of a hill. Mona stopped eating.

'What was that?'

I told her.

She heard a rail outside the house rattle. People hold onto it for support as they walk up the hill. But it was loose.

'And what was *that*?'

We were all quiet.

'I heard something – it's upstairs,' she said.

I went upstairs.

'Nothing,' I said.

'Are you sure?'

'I've got to do this every night,' Oscar said. 'You should see the locks on our doors. And the bolts. And the chains. When I go away after breakfast she locks the double doors with double locks – they're special locks. Then the chains. And then the bolts. She even has a gun and a dog.'

'But what for?' I said.

'I don't know,' Mona said quietly.

'You weren't like that,' I said.

'Let me tell you,' Oscar said, with a sleepy grin. 'You've got some sister.'

Just before nine the farmer and his wife came. And it became a small party. They drank several gins too quickly. They gave us a chicken and pressed tongue. I gave them the bottle of sherry. They left presents for the kids under the tree. They thought it was marvellous to come and find people who had only twenty hours before been in Canada. The farmer's wife – bright-faced, plump – and Mona found something to talk about.

'– I also had my gallstones out.'

'Mine burst,' Mona said, 'as the surgeon was putting it on the tray.'

But they couldn't stay very long as they had to get back to their farm.

Though the room had become much warmer, Oscar had not taken his hat off all evening. He had removed his suit-jacket, sweater, and tie. With his hat on his head he went to sleep in the chair by the fireplace.

As soon as Mona saw that Oscar was asleep she said:

'What do you do about teaching the children religion?'

'We don't,' I said.

'Our kids celebrate Chanukah. They all wear Mogen Dovids around their necks – *This* is the Star of David, Emily,' Mona said, showing her the thin gold chain around her neck. 'In my home I have two sets of dishes. I light the candles on Shabbus. We eat bacon – but outside, in someone else's house. You might think that was hypocritical. Do you light the candles on Friday night?'

'If I did that, Mona, I'd feel hypocritical.'

'Who did you name Rebecca after?' Mona quickly changed the subject.

'After Aunt Rocheh,' I said. 'You may not remember her. She's the one that never married. I think she died when we were kids. How did you get Francine?'

56

'After Fruma – Oscar's grandmother.'

'Fruma is Frieda or Fanny,' I said.

'No,' she said. 'You can take anything from the F's ...'

'But why just the F's ...?' I said.

'Well, it's got to be *like* Fruma – you can have Faith, Felicity, Fawn.'

'They don't sound like Fruma to me.'

'They don't have to sound, long as the first letter's the same. For instance, your Rebecca is after Auntie Rocheh. Then you could have had Roxana, Roxy ...'

'That's the name of a cinema,' I said. 'Who's Lance after?'

'He's after Oscar's grandfather Laybel – he could have been Lawrence, Lorne ...'

'What about Lou or Lionel?'

'They're old-fashioned.'

Mona stubbed out her cigarette and immediately lit up another. I had noticed earlier the area of nicotine on her finger, but it was while I gave her a light that I noticed her hand was shaking.

'We don't let Francine go out with any English boys in Meridian. We send her away to Montreal during the holidays. She also learns Hebrew.'

'Girls in Canada,' I said, 'learn Hebrew?'

'Why not?' Mona said aggressively. 'I believe in God. Don't you?'

'No.'

'Don't *say* that,' Mona said. 'You must *never* say that.'

'Don't believe him,' Emily said, trying to calm her down.

'I believe in fate,' Mona said, 'that between Rosh Hoshannah and Yom Kippur your fate for the year is decided.'

'I don't go along with that,' I said.

No one spoke.

Then Mona chuckled. 'It's a good thing Oscar's asleep, otherwise he'd never forgive me for talking like this.'

We gave them our bedroom. We slept on a mattress in my office with coats over us. This arrangement was all right for tonight. But tomorrow we'd have to try and get some sheets and blankets from the woman next door.

Emily and I were trying to get to sleep. Our eyes seemed level with the gap at the bottom of the door that showed the light from the hall.

'She must have been saving that up for a long time,' Emily said. 'I wanted to like her.'

'I know,' I said. 'I've never felt terrible close to my sister.'

Fifteen years ago, in Montreal, I was asked to leave the middle of an English 10 class.

'Someone to see you,' the Dean's secretary said.

And there in the dark cool hall, under the Arts building clock, was my mother. A bit frightened but dressed nicely in a small blue hat, a new black coat, and dark gloves. She had come up, on her own, from Ottawa to try and make me change my mind about coming to Mona's wedding. I don't know what excuses I gave for not going. And I don't know why I chose my sister's wedding to make a stand.

My mother took me out for a meal, in a small restaurant on St Lawrence Main, which I enjoyed. It wasn't as good as her cooking, but it seemed ages since I had Jewish food. And the signed photographs on the wall of Max Baer, Al Jolson; her, all dressed up, across the table – the food – brought back my childhood on Murray Street; the stillness of the house on the Sabbath, with my mother, a handsome woman, sitting out the afternoons by the window. She wept – she may even have given me a few dollars – and I said I would come.

At the wedding I remember my father coming down the aisle with Mona. He was about the same size as Mona, but looked smaller. In a double-breasted blue serge suit which was cut down to fit him from one of my uncle's discarded suits. His lips pressed tight, near to tears, a little frightened. Away from the house he always looked lost.

Then the reception downstairs in the vestry rooms. There was something like three hundred guests. Most of them I didn't know. Perhaps I had, even then, gone further away from home than I thought. (The way the waiters were openly helping themselves to the booze – the way the people were stuffing themselves.) It seemed to me – at university because of the Veterans' Act, sixty dollars a month, which meant eating peanuts in the last week – that my mother, who had cleaned out her bank account for this wedding, was feeding a lot of strangers.

I remember the young rabbi sitting in front of me, eyes moving continuously. He was new, 'from outa town'. And ate very quickly. Then he got up to make his speech. He talked of Mona, whom he had never seen before.

'Mona, today you are a Princess. Oscar, you are a Prince.'

Earlier that week Princess Elizabeth and the Duke of Edinburgh had got married.

Then he sat down, mumbled quickly and indistinctly his after-eating prayers, gave a few little shakes of his body, and vanished.

Next morning Emily and I and the kids were up early. The kids were very excited. Oscar and Mona came down after ten. Said they slept well. Didn't eat very much but drank endless cups of coffee that Emily kept making and smoked cigarettes.

It was the coldest winter England had for over a century. And though there have been Christmases in this resort where I have been able to walk out without a coat, this time we had fires going in every room. Fortunately our lavatories didn't freeze, though the neighbours' did.

Oscar became a great favourite with the kids. He had a way with children. He sat two of them on one of his knees. He told them stories about Canada and their summer cottage by a lake.

'... we've also got a speedboat and we go through the lakes. You could come and stay at the cottage with us and have some of Mona's blueberry pie and see the animals. You've never seen a skunk? They come right up to the cottage window ...'

He spoke in a sleepy, genial way. The kids loved him.

'Why don't you go back?' he said.

'We'll see – maybe next year.'

'You owe it to the kids,' he said.

Mona began to speak in Yiddish. 'Was it a question of money?' Emily and the kids just looked on, puzzled.

'It's a bit more complicated,' I said in English.

'How about if we take the kids back with us?' Oscar said. 'We'll take Martha and Ella. We'll look after them and they can go and stay with us in the summer at the cottage.'

Martha and Ella were hugging Oscar.

I didn't think for a minute he was serious.

'Look,' Oscar said. 'We can take them back for nothing on our tickets. We'll feed them, look after them. It's not a question of adopting them. They're yours.'

'We'll see,' I said to the two excited kids. It hurt the way they were so willing to go away from us.

Whenever Mona didn't want the kids to understand something she began to talk in Yiddish. Until I finally decided to send the kids into the other room. Only to have Rebecca come back upset.

'They're whispering,' she said. 'They've got secrets.'

It was nearly noon and we hadn't left the kitchen table. I suggested I might take them out, show them the place, and get some fresh air, so as to give Emily a chance to clear up and do some shopping.

It was freezing outside. There was no one out. The puddles in the narrow streets were frozen. The long fine sand beaches were empty. The water in the bay was grey. No boats in the harbour, only a few gulls were huddled together at the harbour's entrance, facing the wind.

'You should see it in the summer,' I said.

'I can imagine,' Mona said, huddled up in her Persian lamb coat. 'It sure is a nice looking place.'

Oscar took coloured moving pictures of Mona and myself and the kids. And of the empty streets, the empty restaurants, the empty beaches, and boarded-up shops. Then we came back with rosy cheeks and sat around the fire in the dining-room.

'It's healthy the fire here,' Mona said, lighting up a cigarette. 'Not like our place – so stuffy.'

I went outside in the courtyard with the coal-bucket and came back with it full to the top.

'You know what you remind me,' Mona said, 'you coming in like that – with the pail of coal?'

'I know,' I said. 'Paw.'

There were times when I went out to get the coal from the shed in the courtyard that I remembered my father coming up from the cellar in the house on Murray Street, with a bucketful of coal for the Quebec stove in the hall. Just as there were times, upstairs in my room, when I was making out a list of payments to come, and remembered him and his black book with his list of people owing him money.

'Do you remember you telling me. Don't let boys touch you between *here*,' she drew a line across her neck. 'And *there*.' Another line at the knees. 'And you remember when you were at university and I saw you in Montreal. You had written that song. When you met me you gave me twenty dollars. I said no. What, you said, it's not enough. And gave me another twenty.'

I didn't remember either of these.

Instead. I remembered when she was about eight or nine. When she was hit with a stone from a slingshot. It cut her head. They had to shave her head. And she wore a beret. She wore it in school. And the kids made fun of her.

'And you remember my wedding?' Mona said. 'You remember Betty's fiancé, Sam? He was supposed to take a movie of the reception. But all he took was pictures of Betty ...'

I didn't remember that either. I remembered Mona being sick. The doctor came to examine her. He gave her a large bar of chocolate for being a good girl. She gave me some. And we went upstairs and ate it in her room. Later, I watched the long, thin, white-yellow worms come out of her mouth and lie slowly twisting on the floor.

* * *

Mona and Oscar had never seen Christmas before except in the movies. So I briefed them.

'This is the way it's going to be tomorrow. We wake up in the morning. We say Happy Christmas to each other. Then the kids come down. We have breakfast. Then go into the front room. And I read out the names and give out the presents.'

When they heard this they went out and came back loaded with presents that they wrapped up in their room and put under the tree.

'I arranged for a taxi to come on Boxing Day,' I said. 'We'll drive around and see some of the country around here.'

'I thought you told Maw you had a jalopy.'

'I might have said that,' I said, 'for Maw's sake.'

In the evening we sat around and watched television.

'They've got the same programmes here,' Mona said, 'as we've got in Meridian.'

'They're American shows,' I said.

We watched a quiz for children. 'Your TV is so much better than ours,' Mona said. 'It's so educational.'

But they were mainly interested in the commercials.

After the news I switched off and we sat around the fire, drank coffee, and smoked cigarettes.

'Why don't you go back to Canada?' Oscar said.

'It takes money to get out of here,' I said. 'And maybe, now, I've lived too long away.'

'With your education you could have been a doctor,' Mona said.

'It's true,' she said to Emily.

'But I'm a writer,' I said. 'How many doctors has Canada got – thousands. How many writers? A handful. It's easier to be a doctor than a writer.'

'Yeh, I know,' Mona said sadly. 'But it's hard.'

I went and got some whisky – no one joined me.

'In a year's time I figure I'll make enough money to retire,' Oscar said.

'Talk, talk,' Mona said. 'That's easy.'

'You'll see if I don't,' Oscar said. 'I'd be half way there if it wasn't for her operations. You know, she's had half a dozen already.'

'It's true,' Mona said.

Oscar I knew was in the scrap-metal business. But he bought anything that he could sell at a profit. He would fill up his warehouse and then load up a truck and drive the stuff to Montreal or Toronto and sell it.

'I've got to ring her up *every* night,' Oscar said, 'when I'm away from Meridian.'

'We've got a system where we don't have to pay,' Mona said. 'If we don't want to talk but just let the other one know that he arrived in Montreal or Toronto – Oscar asks person-to-person and makes up some name like Johnson. "May I speak to Mr Johnson," he says. And I say, "I'm sorry Mr Johnson is not in." And I know he got there all right.'

'You think *that's* something,' Oscar said. 'We know a woman who rings up Montreal long distance to get her kosher meat. She'd call up the butcher and say. 'Is Chuck in?' And of course the man would say that Chuck wasn't in. But he knew that meant she wanted chuck that week.'

'We've got three properties in Meridian,' Mona said. 'So you could come and stay there. I know it's a small out-of-the-way place. But until you find your feet.'

'Thanks,' I said.

But I didn't see much point in exchanging one small town for another. I desperately wanted to get out of this seaside town and live in London again. It's a cosmopolitan city that I miss. I try to go to London as often as I can, but it's expensive. Even so, a few days in London and I come back as if I had a shot in the arm. I feel sharper in London. I go through the streets and feel like singing. I do sing. I go to bed in London feeling slim and not the way I feel here, as if I'm carrying a large body with lots of weight and deadness.

'I've got to get us out,' I told them. 'There are times I've just got to take myself away from here. So I take a train to Plymouth. And just to walk down straight streets again. Until about noon it's fine. After that, I know I've got to come back to this place.'

'Do you miss London, Emily?' Mona said.

'It's my home town. There are days here when I feel life is going by – day after day the same – and you're waiting for something to happen.'

'Like us coming,' Oscar said.

And we all laughed.

On Christmas morning the kids were up early. Emily had filled up their stockings by their beds when they were asleep. And by the time we all came down for breakfast the kids were excited and some of that excitement went over to us. We all said Happy Christmas. And after some coffee we went in the front room. It looked cold outside, no snow but the puddles were frozen. Emily had the large open fire blazing away in each room.

I began to call out the presents. The children's first.

'This is for Rebecca from Uncle Oscar and Auntie Mona – I wonder what it is?' And the excited child undid the parcel and showered Mona and Oscar with kisses. 'And who's this for —?'

Martha, just over nine, got a toilet set from them. There were things for cleaning her nails, plucking her eyebrows, putting on nail polish, and some perfume. The others got the most expensive dolls in the place. I know, I saw them in the store window. It embarrassed Emily more than it did me. There were boxes of candies from Emily's relations, reading-books, and colouring-books for the children, toys, bits of jewellery, and soap, and lots of handkerchiefs.

Around two we sat around the table in the dining-room, all seven of us, for dinner. Emily brought in the turkey. 'It's nearly twelve pounds,' I said. And all the kids said Ah and looked excited.

'You think that's big,' Oscar said to the kids. 'If you come to Canada you'll have turkeys twice that size. You remember,' he said to Mona, 'the turkey we had that time?'

'Canadian turkeys are a little bigger,' Mona said politely.

On the last night we were sitting around the fire, watching some play on television. I decided to switch off. I went out to get some more coal in the bucket. When I came back Oscar was saying:

'... one thing we got for sure. A place in the ground. It's six feet long, three feet wide.' He moved his hand as if he was measuring. 'And six feet deep.'

I noticed Emily getting flushed. She turned her head away from Oscar. 'Stop it. Stop it,' she said quietly.

'It's all the same,' Oscar went on taking no notice. 'We'll all have it in the end.'

Emily turned her head away from us all. 'I'm sorry,' she said. And, weeping, got up and went out of the room.

Mona and Oscar looked astonished.

'Is she upset?' Mona said.

'No,' I said, sarcastically.

'She's got to accept this, you know,' Oscar said. 'It's no use running away.'

'She doesn't accept it,' I said.

'But we all got to die,' my sister said.

'I think,' I said, 'you brought back her father.'

'So?' Oscar said. ' I buried my mother.'

'Maybe you better go and speak to her,' Mona said.

I went back. Emily had stopped crying, although her face looked as if she hadn't. I put my arms around her and kissed her.

'I'm sorry,' she said. And I kissed her again.

'It was a lot of things. It was suddenly as if I realized that she, they, being a Jew. As if I was an outsider and we weren't close, man and woman, like we are when she goes on talking Jewish. This is my house she's in and I suddenly felt we'll die and they are able to believe in something – that you are part of, and I'm not. And there isn't anything I could do about it.'

I kissed her again. 'Let's go back in.'

We did.

'I'm sorry,' Emily said.

'He's going to put us all in a story,' Mona said, 'just watch.'

'I don't care,' Oscar said. Then turning to me. 'If you can make a buck out of it – that's OK with me.'

I phoned up London and fixed them up with a room in the Strand Palace. 'It's so much with a bath and so much without,' I said.

'We'll have without,' Mona said.

They were going to London because Oscar wanted to do a round-up of some of the places he knew when he was a soldier over here in the war.

'I'll cry when I say goodbye,' Mona said. 'I don't know why. I'm not like him. I'm like Paw. I cry.'

We had to wait for the train at the station. Mona looked at Oscar. And Oscar put out his hand to shake mine.

I felt a piece of paper in my palm. I looked and saw it was a five pound note.

'Thanks,' I said, and gave it back to him. Since two of the kids were with us there was no scene.

'My pocket is deeper than yours,' Oscar said, still holding the note out for me.

I put my hand in my coat-pocket. Then put my hand in his pocket.

'It *is* deeper,' I said.

Then the train came. I went in with their luggage and got them an empty compartment and kissed my sister. She wept, without a sound, her face screwed up. And I thought how like my father she looked. I shook hands and embraced Oscar.

They rang up that night to say they got in OK and the room was fine, the hotel was fine, and a blizzard was on. I told them to go to Blooms in Whitechapel for a meal.

Next night Mona spoke to Emily. They decided to go back tomorrow morning. London they found was expensive. ('There are no bargains.') The weather was miserable. And they missed their kids.

On the morning they were to take off, we returned the bedding to our neighbour, cleared the rooms. Nothing had really changed. And again that feeling of being cut off, and the need to get out of here. Luckily one of the payments came through.

So I took myself off to Plymouth. Went to see the new books and the new magazines at W.H. Smiths. Had some coffee and doughnuts at Joe Lyons. Saw a bad movie. Had a meal. And came back.

On the following Monday we got a letter from Mona. On page two she said:

> ... Dad was operated on this morning and it's a good job they did as both doctors said he wouldn't have lasted four months. I never saw such a big stone that he had in his bladder. The doctor said he got through better than average. We saw and spoke to him but he was in pain and got his hypo so thought we had better leave so he could rest. Poor Mom she looks terrible and it's taking a lot out of her. As soon as I hear anymore will let you know.

On January 22nd came another letter.

> It has been sometime since we heard from you and hope all is well. Saw Dad yesterday afternoon and he got his stitches out and is looking better. I saw the doctor and asked him how he is getting along and he said as well as can be expected. Dad seems confused at times though. We brought the children yesterday and he was happy to see them. He's well looked after.

February 2nd, Meridian.

> Hope all is well with you. Haven't been down to see Dad the last while and everytime I speak to Mom she seemed upset so yesterday afternoon I got my cleaning woman to watch the children and went down to see him. I also saw the doctor. He says Dad is coming along but is confused and that he doesn't know if he'll get better. He wants to put him in a rest home if he can get him in. The other day he went out in his pyjamas and it was below zero. I don't think he realizes he is in hospital. He recognizes us all but talks as if we were still living on Murray Street and gets confused.

February 25th, Meridian.

> Dad was moved to the nursing home on Friday and went

down yesterday to see him. He seems much happier and I don't know if he realizes where he is or not. At night they put a restrainer on him so he won't get out. Thursday morning at the hospital they found him outside at the Parking Lot. It was his fourth time out.

March 10th, Meridian.

Hope all is well and what's the matter I haven't heard from you. Saw Dad on Thursday and he was so happy to see me. Apparently he got out again so when I was there the Director of the Nursing Home spoke to me and asked me to tell him not to go out and he got angry with me and said how can I get out as you see I'm lying here.

April 6th, Meridian.

Last week he got out just with his clothes and slippers and the Nursing Home is past the exhibition grounds and he walked to Bank Street and went in a restaurant (he had no money) they gave him a cup of coffee and phoned the Nursing Home and an orderly came with a taxi and got him.

'For some reason he wants to get out,' I said to Emily. 'But once out he doesn't know what to do. It's at the opposite end of town from where we live. He doesn't know how to get home from there. I don't know why, but I'm proud of him running away like this ...' tears were coming to my eyes. And with Mona's letter I went upstairs to my room. There was the sign *You've got to get out of here* facing me on the wall. The mirror with the postcards.

I went to the window. It overlooked a small valley of cottages. There was a funeral taking place in the street immediately below. The hearse with the glass sides had driven up outside a small stone cottage. Men in black brought out the light wood coffin. And heaped it with bright yellow flowers in the hearse. The mourners walked behind it. They seemed to walk like mechanical toys.

I stood at the window, over to the side, so they couldn't see me, and watched them go by.

From this window I have now watched several funerals. They were all of people I didn't know.

Chapter Nine

BECAUSE we hardly see anyone here we are a very close family. This Sunday morning it's raining. I'm up here typing little notes to myself. I can hear the children singing Jerusalem then John Brown's Body. Then Rebecca gets into one of her tempers. 'You're a pig,' she shouts at Emily. 'I hate you. You're always teasing me. You're all horrible. Pig. Pig.' And I can hear her going noisily up the stairs into her room and closing the door. 'I'm going to kill myself now.'

Emily comes up the stairs. 'Rebecca, open the door.'

'Leave me alone.'

'I'm asking you to open the door.'

'Leave me alone.'

'Rebecca I want to speak to you.'

'Leave me alone.'

Emily goes down the stairs. Then I hear sobbing. A few minutes later she opens the door and comes over and kisses Emily. 'I'm sorry,' she said quietly. She comes over and kisses me. 'I'm sorry.'

She had to be carried on her first day at school. She wouldn't go. I had to carry her, legs kicking, people in the street watched. Last night when I went to the toilet I could hear she was crying. I went to her room.

'I can't go to sleep,' she said. 'I'm scared.'

'Why are you scared. Is it something you read?'

'No. It's what I heard at the playground.'

'You don't have to believe what other children say.'

'But when I go to sleep I don't know what to think about. I try to think of good things so I'll have pleasant dreams. Then these bad things come. And I'm scared. I hear noises.'

'Where?'

'From the walls.'

'It's only Miss Benson next door.'

'But I hear noises above.'

'It's the rain.'

We were both quiet listening to the rain on the window.

'You can go now,' she said softly. 'I can go to sleep.'

I left the room with the animal pictures on the wall; the

wooden crate filled with books; the piece of paper saying it was her club and it had one rule, 'You must keep your promise.'

One time she got into another of her tempers. 'You're all horrible.' She shouted. 'I hate you. I'll run away from you all.' And locked herself in her room and wouldn't come out. I began to shout at her to open the door. I tried to force the door open. It held. Emily and the other two were in tears. We went into different rooms visibly upset.

For several minutes the house was silent.

Then I began to hear buzz ... buzz buzz ... A high pitched sound was going through the house. Buzz buzz ... buzz buzz ... It was coming from behind Rebecca's locked door. She had a toy morse code thing. She didn't know how to make words. She was just sending buzz ... buzz buzz ... Tapping out messages from behind her locked door saying she was sorry.

Ella has the nicest nature. A pretty child with blonde hair, small features. She wants to go to Africa or to India to look after the children. She is saving up pennies and sending them to Save the Children Fund. Every Monday at school she has to write her news. She wrote that she had a boyfriend in America. The teacher marked that excellent. She wrote that she got a new two-wheeler bike at home. 'It is red. I like it very much. I ride it a lot of times.' Again she was marked excellent and told she was an imaginative child. On her seventh birthday she asked Emily if she could have a birthday party this year. Emily said, 'We'll see.'

When it came I didn't have money. Emily said: 'We'll have a nice tea, all of the family, but we can't ask anybody.' Ella went and made invitations. She made drawings of a birthday cake with lots of candles and everyone looked happy. She gave the invitations to Emily, myself, Rebecca and Martha. The childish lettering said: 'My party will be a happy one if you will come to it.' She enters all kinds of competitions hoping to win a bicycle, a car, a house. She has a new friend, Catherine. She came back from spending Saturday there and described the nice new house. 'We had to take off our shoes inside the door and go in our stockings so we wouldn't hurt the floors.' She was brought back by car. Then it is our turn to have the child here. Emily hopes it will go all right. That the child will not fall out with ours because the house isn't as smart.

Martha is sentimental and bossy. She cries easily. She is also very anxious. If we have to go anywhere she begins to worry long before the time. When Rebecca is in one of her tempers she wants to give in to her so there won't be any unpleasantness in the house. One hot summer day I saw her with a school friend at the edge of the beach. They were sending out messages in glass bottles. She also has these 'voices' as she calls them. They're just accents she puts on. There is her deep one – real deep like she was eighty or something. And there is her Welsh voice. 'So you're going down the mine, bach.' And there is her Liverpool voice. That makes us all laugh. 'I do my voices for company,' she said. The three of them have pen pals. In Norway, in France, in Canada.

I can hear Emily asking Rebecca. 'Whatever happened to you poor child?'

'I sneezed,' Rebecca said.

'Lunch is ready,' Martha called out.

'Coming,' I said.

Chapter Ten

I HAD a visit this morning from a Canadian academic. He was over here on a fellowship doing research on Emily Carr. He had been told Emily Carr lived for a short while in Carnbray and thought he would see what kind of place it was. And being down here he said he thought he'd call in. He said his name was Frank Sincere. Hard to believe until I remember some of the odd names I knew in Canada.

As we passed the local small library he went in and walked straight to the index file system.

'It's the first thing I do when I go to a new place,' he said going through the cards. 'See if any of my books are in the library.'

None were. I don't know why he expected them to be since his books were only published in Canada.

He was a mixture of arrogance ('Do you think they'll want my autograph?') and humility ('Back home, I'm a big fish in a little pond'). He had a craggy North American face with grey hair crew cut and hairy ears. He told me he went to a conference in London. 'A female British academic invited me back to her flat. She tried to seduce me. But I couldn't. She had a moustache.'

'Maybe that's what girls are wearing this year.'

He wanted to know if there was 'any good stuff' around here. I walked him down to the front. Past the peepshows, the slot machines, the picture postcards. It was the beginning of September and the last of the summer tourists were about. We stood by the silver harbour rails and watched some blonde girls on the sandy beach.

'In London,' he said, 'I went to a strip club and saw the most extraordinary sight. A blind man was let in. Now why would someone blind come into a strip joint? I've been thinking about it ever since. It bothers me.'

A red sports car stopped near us, its motor running. A blonde girl, dressed in white, with a good tan, was at the wheel. Watching the girl, I thought of the car doing a strip. First the wheels were discarded, then the lights came off, then the body, then the steering wheel ...

71

In Fore Street he saw, in an Arts and Crafts window, a glass container filled with yellow coloured water and some wax. A light was at the bottom. And as the wax was heated it rose slowly in the liquid changing into different shapes. When the wax rose further it cooled and fell back forming other shapes. Then it rose again. He was fascinated by this. Watched it for several minutes.

'Somebody could have got a ph.d. with this,' he said. It was his highest tribute.

I showed him more of the front then walked along the far pier. Then around the narrow streets of the old part, then up the slopes to the wealthy residential section. Looking back we could see the blue of the bay glistening in the sun, the white of the lighthouse, the delicate yellow, green, orange-brown of the far shore fields.

'Isn't the world a marvellous place. For rich people. I bet,' he said, 'you thought I made that up.'

'Who did?'

'Somerset Maugham. I know another good one. See if you can guess. Life being what it is one dreams of revenge.'

'I give up.'

'Nietzche,' he said.

We walked back a different way. By the hotels, the large houses. I took him around the terraces on top of the slopes and then back through the small narrow streets to the beaches and the front.

'You've seen just about all of Carnbray,' I said as we rested against the harbour rails and watched sand eels swim by the harbour wall.

'I feel there's something important that I have missed.'

So I told him how it is sometimes early in the morning. The gulls very loud as you walk through empty streets. The fresh morning air. A red streak on the water and red in the glass of the windows along the front. I told him what it was like, in summer, at dusk when the anchored French Crabbers are vivid and sharp on the flat white-blue water of the bay. And the far shore fields, the terraces, the wet sand, are seen through a pink haze.

'I thought you hated this place,' he said.

'But I do,' I said.

Next morning at 8:30 he dropped in to say goodbye. He had

large boxes of chocolates for the children. And for Emily, two dozen small pink roses with dark green stems. I walked him back to the railway station.

'Did you get anything out of Carnbray?'

'There's nothing here,' he said. 'It looks nice on the outside. But when you look at it closely – there's nothing here. It just goes through your fingers.'

Chapter Eleven

YOU FEEL the inertia of this place most during the winter months. The summer restaurants are closed, shops are empty, the For Sale signs are up. Wherever you walk you feel you are walking by empty rooms. The side streets are also empty. Women with aprons come out of their cottages to shake table-cloths on the road for the birds. And in the morning it is still dark when the children go to school. On blustery days the windows make a noise. As does the line of bamboo outside the back window. From the front window I can see white caps in the bay, the long swell, and a dull brown freighter riding it out. When I go to the post office and come back the long way – through the main street to get some exercise and fresh air – I see the small signs of anxiety of the shopkeepers in the way they watch prospective customers.*

It was during this time that Anna Likely came into our lives. On the afternoon of January 22nd she stood outside the front door with a small middle-aged man and a boy of about seven. She wore an apricot coat.

'Joseph Grand?'

'Yes,' I said.

'Albert told us to look you up,' the man said. 'My name is Walter Likely, this is my wife Anna, his name is Leon

I asked them in.

Although I react to people physically and I liked immediately both Anna and Walter, I have always found it difficult to describe people. Put me in front of a landscape – a walk down to the front, the Crabbers in the bay, the harbour when the

---

*But there are also the warm winter days. When the far shore looks so close – you can see miles down the coast. When people come out to the sun like flies and sit against the stone and the wet sand and smell the salt and the seaweed and walk along the tide-line. Some children paddle and this is January and the sun is as hot as June. And there is something about these fine still winter days that brings a terrible longing. It is almost a physical feeling in the stomach. The pace is slow, as the surf coming in.

tide is out, the far shore fields – and I feel immediately at home. But with people I am faced with a lack of confidence. (Perhaps because I know you can never tell enough about one person.) Of course there are the externals. Anna had straggling dark hair that kept going into the side of her face. She would keep pushing it away from her eyes. Her eyes were her best feature. The mouth became a bit crooked when she talked. And she didn't have much chin, which she tried to hide and which was an endearing quality of hers. She also had this soft voice that wavered a bit. You would have to come close to hear. Or else she would come close to you. She did this not only with men. I remember how Emily was taken with her. 'I'd like to be like Anna,' she said, after they had gone – but that is going ahead.

I helped Anna off with her coat. And indicated that she ought to come into the dining-room where Emily and the kids were sitting by the fire. But Anna refused to move.

'There's a cat.'

'It's only a kitten,' said Emily.

'I can't stand cats,' Anna said. 'You must take it out,' she appealed to me.

I picked up the black kitten and brought it out in the court.

After that things were all right. Of course they didn't know Albert. They met him at some party. Walter told him they were coming down near Carnbray to get away from the London winter. Albert gave them our address.

'We rented a cottage in Weston,' Walter said. 'We took it for a month. This is the last week.'

'Do you like it here?'

'I've felt sleepy all the time,' Anna said.

'It's the air,' I said.

What Walter told Albert was only part of the reason for leaving London. The other was to treat Anna to a holiday. In April she was opening in *The Wood Demon*. It was the first time Anna would be acting in the West End.

'I'm Elena,' she said. 'Do you know the play?'

'No,' I said.

'Every night,' Walter said, 'she goes to bed with Chekhov and a hot water bottle.'

We all went into the kitchen and sat around the table to have tea. The children were as excited as we were in seeing new faces, and such handsome ones. They talked happily and loudly. Walter told me, above the children's voices, that he had an estate office in south-east London. He wanted to know what rent we were paying. 'Three pounds ten a week,' I said. He thought we'd have to pay at least five times more in London for this kind of house.

Suddenly Walter shouted: 'We'll have a silence period.'

The talking stopped.

Their boy blushed. Our kids looked to us, bewildered. No one spoke.

Finally Anna said. 'Walter likes to have these silence periods.'

And I detected in her voice a quality I hadn't noticed before – something that sounded close to despair.

'It's good for discipline,' Walter said to me, as if no one else was listening. 'They need to know who is in charge.'

After that it took a little while to talk freely again. But they couldn't stay long. They had to drive back to Weston. We asked them over for tomorrow evening and suggested that they spend the night here.

They came on Friday just after eight. Walter had a bottle of brandy for us and a box of Lucky Numbers for the kids. I told him they were already in bed. When he came down I went up to close their light.

'Walter told us such a good story,' Ella said. 'It was about a butterfly that was very beautiful.'

'No more candies tonight,' I said and kissed them.

'Hope you have a nice sleep and pleasant dreams,' Rebecca said, quickly, as she did every night.

'Same to you.'

'Thank you.'

'Daddy,' Martha said. 'Aren't they nice.'

'Yes,' I said.

When I came downstairs the other guest had arrived. We invited Clara, a retired doctor of thirty-nine who had not long come down here. Her husband George sold advertising for various British periodicals. For eight months of the year he was away from England. And after ten years of living in hospital quarters he had saved enough to buy her a house in the fashionable part of Carnbray. They were going to put down roots. Clara would not work but look after their two children.

Perhaps it was because George was away or perhaps Clara had worked and lived in hospitals too long. Whatever it was, Clara did not know what to do with herself in Carnbray. I saw her walking along the deserted front dressed in purple tights, pink shoes, a green leather coat. Another time, in one of those long dresses that were fashionable just after the war, with a large hat, as if she was going to a garden party. Emily told me how Clara had come up to her in the street. 'Guess what I've done? I was so crazy with boredom last night I picked out all my eyebrows.'

'Have you heard from George?'* I asked. And saw him, the only man in Carnbray, with his camel-hair coat, his Russian kind of fur cap, the silver-topped stick ... walking beside the terraced houses, the grey cottages, the empty Bed and Breakfast signs. A kind of dandified figure, if you didn't know him. Like Clara, like us, out of place here.

'I had a letter last week,' Clara said. 'From Peru.'

I thought she and the Likelys might get on for they both had lived in Glasgow and were Catholics.

'You know,' Walter said. 'You remind me of Mary MacKenzie, or is it Sara White?'

'They're hideous,' Clara said in disgust. 'Mary MacKenzie is the ugliest woman I ever saw. She reminds me of Beethoven.'

When Clara is uncomfortable with people she starts to clown. This time she mussed her black hair, took out a pencil, put it under her nose, curled her top lip around it so that only the top lip held it.

She said to Walter: 'I bet, to you, I look like Hitler.'

'No. Like a Fiji Islander.'

This annoyed Clara even more.

I went out of the front room and up the stairs to see if the kids were all right. I had come down to the first floor, I was on the landing, when I saw Anna quietly closing the door of the small room where the boy was sleeping. She must have come up for the same purpose. She saw me. And quickly walked

---

*George liked Carnbray so much he told me he was going to stay here the rest of his life. But he only stayed the autumn. A few years later George and Clara divorced.

over. She came very close, her mouth a little open.

'I love you,' she said and raised her mouth.

We kissed.

She undid the two buttons of my shirt and put a hand inside and moved it over my chest. I didn't know if she was doing this to find out whether I had hair on my chest. Feeling I ought to do something similar I put a hand on her skirt where her belly was and gently rubbed it.

'I could tell,' she said, 'when you took my coat off and held my hand.'

I didn't remember holding her hand.

We kissed again.

'I love you,' she said.

I wasn't in love with her then. I have found that women who are attractive and also intelligent make me feel uncertain. And in order to be sexually aroused I have found it necessary to feel, in some way, superior to the woman. Anna understood this. Because later I noticed something calculated about her helplessness. It had a strange vitality about it. But that is going ahead. All I remember at the top of the landing was thinking how nice this was, that I was forty and she only twenty-six, and that she kissed very gently.

Back in the front room we behaved as if nothing had happened. Although our eyes would meet and hold before moving elsewhere. I saw Clara home. The street lights were out. We walked on the road. I kept looking to the sky to get the turnings. Clara didn't like Walter or Anna.

'She's just a peasant. I've known hundreds like her.'

I took it that Clara was jealous.

Walter was out of the room when I got back. Emily and Anna were sitting by the low fire. Emily told Anna that she felt tired, would she excuse her if she went to bed.

I saw Anna blush.

'You're so old-fashioned,' she said. And brought her hands quickly to her cheeks.

As soon as Emily left the room Anna came over. We kissed.

'I could hardly sit here with you across the room.'

'Walter will be coming down.'

'We can hear him.'

When we heard footsteps we separated. And when Walter came into the room Anna was sitting in a chair on one side of the fire and I was standing on the other.

Walter said. 'It's getting late Anna. We ought to go to bed.'

She went with Walter into our bed. Emily and I were in the next room on a mattress on the floor. When I entered to lie beside Emily she was asleep.

Next morning Emily got up early and left the room to get everyone's breakfast.

As soon as Emily had gone out Anna came in. She knelt on the mattress. She wanted to be kissed.

'I haven't brushed my teeth.'

'What does that matter,' she said.

'I'll come up to London.'

'Come and stay with us,' she said. 'I'll bring you breakfast in bed.'

We kissed again. She made no move to leave. I thought this was madness. Emily could come in. Or one of the kids. 'I'll get dressed,' I said. 'I'll see you downstairs.'

I don't remember breakfast. But afterwards I remember Anna asking the kids for their handkerchiefs and emptying a lot of her Arpege into the handkerchiefs. Then we found ourselves alone in the kitchen. We kissed by the gas stove.

'Someone is coming,' she said.

'The kettle is boiling.'

'How do you make tea?'

'I put the tea leaves in, then the boiling water.'

'Don't you warm the pot — Hello Walter,' I said. 'I can't make tea.'

'Neither can Anna,' Walter said.

'Because he spent his youth in India,' she said, 'Walter thinks he's the only one who knows how to make tea. It's a ceremony with him. The kettle has to be just on the boil. Then quickly poured in. Then he brings the teapot into the room wrapped in towels.'

I thought then she wasn't an actress for nothing.

We all had tea and biscuits. The closed windows steamed up. Walter was drawing funny faces with a finger on the glass for the children. And Anna was admiring some chives that Emily had in a tall glass. They had gone to seed. They looked very pretty, delicate mauve ball-like flowers on long green stems. I decided to get everyone out of the house. It would be better just to be outside in the open.

We walked to the front. It began to rain. The tide was in. And where the water covered the sand the sand looked pale green. We walked past the amusement arcade, the summer cafés, the bric-à-brac shops, the paperback place. Nothing was open. A sign outside the Salvation Army said:

Fed up with the futility of things!
Looking for something worth living for?
Then why not give God a chance.

Beside the white customs house the toy shop was closed but I could see a man moving a wooden crate filled with straw. On impulse I went in and got their boy a green Dinky jeep and ours some farm animals. When I came out I saw Anna. She looked miserable, like a wet bird.

Back in the house she insisted that the kitten be put out again. I took it out. It began to meow. One of the kids must have taken pity on it. For when I came out to the hall I saw Anna and the boy start to come down the stairs. Then stop. Anna saw the kitten at the bottom.

'Darling,' she hugged the boy to her side. 'Save me from this *monster.*'

She liked to do things all the time like that. Always making ordinary things into drama.

They left early in the afternoon. I don't know what Emily and Anna talked about when they were together. But after they had gone Emily said. 'I'd like to be like her.' Then later in the evening. 'I like Anna. I know we can be good friends.'

Sunday after lunch the phone rang.
'Hello.'
'Is there anyone there?'
'There's no one. Emily has taken the kids for a walk.'
'Have you missed me?'
'Yes. Where are you?'
'I don't know. I'm all out of breath. I told Walter I was going for a walk. I've walked miles trying to find a kiosk. Have you missed me?'
'Yes. When can I see you?'
'I'll arrange something. But we must be careful. Walter can be so cruel.'

I didn't like her then. Perhaps because I like loyalty in others. And I nearly said something – I don't know why I didn't. Possibly because even now I couldn't take what was happening very seriously. I still thought of it as a kind of game. A bit of excitement (lust and curiosity) for me. And something the same for her. Even later, on the Monday, when I was with her alone for a few minutes as we were walking over some rocks ... I asked her to come away with me on the Continent. She said she'd like to but there was the boy. I knew, even as I asked her, that this was what I should be saying at this time. In any case I recognized it for the bravado it was. I didn't have enough money for a decent hotel in London, let alone the Continent for two.

'Can I write to you?'

'Yes,' I said. 'Write to Barclays Bank.'

'I'll write.'

'When?'

'Soon as I get back. You'll have a letter tomorrow. I've done nothing but think of you.'

Next morning I went to the bank, a place I don't like going as I was overdrawn.

'Is there a letter for me?' I asked the bald teller.

'Yes,' he said.

He gave me Anna's letter. I saw it was open. The gum still good. All this secrecy and she forgot to seal the envelope. It seemed the sort of action a criminal would do. I walked with the letter down to the front. And read it standing against the rails by the ladies' lavatory. 'I can get through to you,' she wrote. 'With other men I can't'

I put the letter in my back pocket and walked along the empty front. I felt excited and happy. As though I was experiencing something I thought I had lost. Something that belonged to my youth.

Next day we took the bus to Weston. They had rented an old square cottage. It was a typical summer-let place, the furniture picked up at auction sales. The only bit of gaiety was a postcard of a Renoir landscape above the mantel.

'From one of my admirers,' Anna said to Emily.

'She has many admirers,' Walter said.

Before lunch we went to the small harbour, climbed along the rocks, to find rock pools for the kids. Anna took my hand as we scrambled over a slab of granite.

'I got your letter,' I said. 'I'll be in Penzance tomorrow.'

'Keep talking,' Walter called out. And I saw he was taking our picture.

'I'll let you know how we can meet,' she said as we posed for the photograph.

Next day the phone rang. Emily answered. 'It's the bank manager. He wants to talk to you. Has a cheque bounced?'

'I don't know. Hello.'

'Mr Grand this is Speed here. I had a call from Mrs Likely. She said could you meet her at seven p.m. outside the library in Penzance.'

'Thanks.'

'And there's a letter for you.'

'I'll be right over.'

'What did he want?' Emily said.

'Nothing. I forgot to sign one of the cheques. I better go and do it now.'

At lunch I told Emily I had to go into Penzance to be revaccinated for my trip to Canada, then see an insurance man because I was flying. A bit of luck had come. A colour supplement asked me to go to Canada before the end of March and do two articles on Montreal and the province of Quebec. Allowing for expenses, I'd be about three hundred pounds to the good. I also told Emily that a French film was on and I would take that in.

The revaccination took a few minutes. The insurance a bit longer. The man grasped my hand in a funny way when I came in. He must have been a freemason. If I gave the right squeeze back I probably would have got a reduction. From the freemason I went to see a film. It was about call girls in Paris who went under a cover of delivering flowers. But I kept looking at the clock in the back. I left a half hour early. And made my way to the library on Morrab Road with the cannon in the wooden holder. At the bottom of the road was the sea, black, with the gentle moving light of a small boat in it.

Impatient, I began to walk back when I saw Anna coming. She had on the apricot coat and a red beret.

'I came in early,' I said.

'So did I. I've been watching a film.'

'About call girls?'

82

'Yes.'

'We were both in there.'

And we laughed. A thing neither of us did much while we were together.

I didn't know where to walk. For some reason we were both nervous. I took the first turning. A passage between buildings. We kissed. There was a trace of Arpege on her. Then arm in arm walked further down.

'It's dark,' she said. 'Do you know where we are?'

'Yes. Near the Gardens. An old cinema used to be here.'

We stopped and kissed awkwardly. I tried to think where we could go.

'I told Walter I was going in to have my hair done then to see a film,' she said. 'I think he is becoming suspicious.'

'I told Emily that I was going in for a revaccination. I don't think she suspects anything.'

We came out to the promenade. And walked into the first pub. A small room with a coal fire going. The walls were painted railway brown, they had photographs of old rugby teams. Apart from the man behind the bar there was no one in.

'What would you like?'

'I'll have a light ale,' she said.

I came back with two light ales.

'Write me a letter,' she said. 'Give it to me when we come tomorrow night.'

'All right. I'll come up to London.'

'When?'

'In ten days.'

'On Tuesday?'

'Yes.'

'Will you stay with Albert?'

'Yes.'

'You'll have a letter waiting when you arrive. But we must be careful. If Walter finds out he can be so cruel. The last time he found I was seeing someone he wouldn't talk to me for two months. I had to go and see a psychiatrist. What's the time?'

'Ten to nine.' And I didn't like the part about the psychiatrist.

'I'll have to go in twenty minutes.'

'Why so early?'

'The last bus leaves at 9:15. If I'm not on it Walter will guess.'

And the way she said it depressed me.

'I don't want to go,' she said.

I didn't say anything.

'Why are you staring?' she said.

'I just want to look at your face.'

'You're embarrassing me.'

We were holding hands.

'I won't ever forget you – Joseph.'

And I knew it was over then.

We had another drink then left the pub and walked arm in arm beside what used to be a harbour but now was half-filled in for a car park. In the small depressions, of the gravel and sand, water glistened.

'I'll see you tomorrow night.'

We kissed lightly.

I watched her cross the road and get into the waiting bus. She sat by a window on the side facing me. She didn't move or wave or smile. I watched the small green bus go up the slope to Market Jew Street. Then I walked to the one black taxi by the railway station.

'How much is it to Carnbray?'

'Thirty bob.'

'Will you take a cheque?'

When I got back I didn't have to lie to Emily right away. A middle-aged woman that I vaguely recognized was sitting by the fire with Emily. She heard I was going to Canada and wanted to know if I could trace her husband. I said I wouldn't be in Canada long enough for that.

The Likelys came next evening for a farewell drink. Perhaps I only imagined the awkwardness. But it began, earlier, in the morning. I was up in this room trying to write a letter to Anna. She had written me a couple of 'love' letters. I felt I had to write one back. I also knew that the thing down here had come to an end. And I was looking forward to London. Perhaps it would be different once I was up there. I don't know why I didn't come right out and say: 'We have begun something. We can go on from here.' Instead I fell back on the kind of letter I wrote to Emily in the few months before we were married when she lived with her parents. I even used the same phrases. They meant something once. Now they seemed so embarrassingly romantic and derivative. I had the letter in an envelope in my back pocket. And early in the evening I went out from the front room, into the hallway, and put the letter in one of the pockets of her coat. Then returned to the front room. A few minutes later I watched Anna get up and leave the room. Then I heard her walking up the stairs.

Walter was saying. 'You must get out. It's just too easy to go to seed down here.'

'I've been telling him that for a long time,' Emily said.

Anna came back into the room.

'When we get back,' Walter said, 'I'll look around in my office. I'll try to get you something near us.'

Emily was delighted.

They didn't stay long. They were leaving early in the morning and they said they still had some packing to do. At the door I shook Walter's hand. We watched them go down the front steps and walk to their car when Anna stopped and turned around. I thought she had forgotten something. She came back to kiss Emily.

During the next week I had three letters from Anna at the bank. After I read them I burned them. And though I slept with Emily I would say I was tired or pretend I wanted to do some work at night. So when I did come to bed she was asleep. I wondered about Anna and Walter. When, in one letter, she wrote how much better Walter felt because of the holiday and that he was 'in good form'. I found I was jealous.

I wanted to tell someone about Anna. But who was there. Only Jimmy. I walked over to his place. And found him all on his own.

'Thank God you've come,' he said. 'I don't know what to do with myself. Let's go for a ride.'

I thought how could Jimmy feel cut off. He belongs here, he's rich, he's got lovely grounds, nice house, two cars.

He drove along the coast road with neat green fields against the blue sea on the right. The moor on the left, large haunches of earth with granite boulders sticking out of the earth. I was going to tell him about Anna. But what was there to talk of? Instead I listened to him tell me about being isolated. 'We all have to go through this isolation,' he said. 'We all have to see it through.' Then he told me about a trip he was making to America in six weeks, how he was looking forward to that. I told him I was going up to London. And while there I would see Anna.

'She's all right,' he said.

And I remembered Jimmy coming in for only a short while, one drink, during the Likelys' first night at the house. And how he and Anna kissed good night at the door when he was leaving.

He stopped the car near a pub. We walked along the path. He picked up a stone and threw it at a telegraph pole. He missed, but he was feeling better.

On Monday I took the night train up. It got in just before seven next morning. I washed and shaved, on the train, in Paddington Station. Then took a taxi to Lyons in Piccadilly and had bacon and eggs and coffee. Then another taxi to Albert's flat.

'Hullo old boy. Nice to see you. How is Emily, the children?'

'They're well.'

He had on his winter windcheater with fur collar, zipped up to the neck. Albert has these small meannesses that would show in things like not having an electric fire on if you could keep warm by wearing extra clothes.

'Where have you been since I last saw you?'

'France, Italy, Poland, Germany, Czechoslovakia. I won't be able to see you much. I've got to do some work.'

'How was Poland?'

'I went to see the places where my father and mother lived. There was nothing there. Someone told me where they shot the Jews of the town. It was only a field. I went and left some flowers and said Kaddish. If you want to see anything of this you'd better go soon otherwise it just won't be there.'

'How about Germany?'

'They're much better than the Poles. The place is humming.'

'What about the business of going to see the Nazi who got off?'

'Let's not talk about that,' he said quietly. 'Let's just forget it. I have to get down to work. I must go. Olga will look after you.'

'Hello sir,' Olga said coming out of the kitchen. She was wearing her winter fur coat. 'Will you have something to eat?'

'I've just had breakfast.'

'A cup of tea?'

We sat by the small table in the kitchen having tea.

'How is Albert?'

'He is sick, sir. One minute he is shouting at me. The next minute he is sorry, he wants to put a pound note in my pocket. Tell him to see a doctor. He quarrel with his brothers.'

'But why?'

'Because they do not want to go to the cemetery every week. He throw them out of the house. Sir, there's a letter for you.'

It was from Anna.

I rang the number. Walter answered. He invited me up next day for lunch.

I took an electric train from Charing Cross and got off at Eltham Well Hall. There were some nice poplars and a laid out formal garden and tennis courts. I turned into their road. I don't know why I was disappointed. Perhaps because I didn't want to see the domestic side. Or perhaps because what I did see was like Emily's background. The semi-detached with the wooden gate in the front, the small garden with a neat privet hedge, the curtains drawn in front to keep the sun from bleaching the furniture.

Walter opened the door and welcomed me in. He took the dozen roses I brought for Anna and I could hear him talking in another room.

Then she came in.

'You shouldn't have done this,' she said, the roses by her face. 'You look smart, Joseph.'

'It's the coat and these shoes,' I said. 'I got them this morning. Listen. The shoes squeak when I walk.'

Getting through lunch was difficult. I could not keep my eyes off Anna. I did get her alone, once, when Walter and the boy happened to be out of the room. And there was a hurried kiss against the sideboard behind the door.

'We must be careful darling,' she said. 'I'll think of something.'

As I was leaving Walter said. 'Give us a ring Joseph if you're at a loose end. Otherwise we'll see you for lunch on Sunday.'

Birds woke me next morning. Then chimes of a clock. I counted six. Then another clock struck six. Then the sound of a large jet overhead. It felt marvellous waking up and finding oneself in London. Albert was also up. He was standing by the door waiting for the postman. I thought it was because I was living in Carnbray – but here was Albert, living in the centre of London, also waiting for letters.

At 9:15 I dialled the Likelys' number.

But it was Walter who answered. He said that Anna had to go to the dentist, but if I was free for lunch he would meet me in town. I said I was tied up having to see the editor of the colour supplement.

I met him in a new glass building and a taxi was waiting. 'We can go to Chez Victor and have a meal,' he said. 'I can sign for it. I come here about twice a week. Sometimes I take my starving friends and sign names like Graham Greene, Stephen Spender ...' I wondered what name he would sign for me. When the bill came, he said. 'Oh, you're a contributor. It's all right.'

Afterwards I picked up a cheque for £200 as an advance on the Canadian articles. I sent £100 to Emily and with the balance I decided to move from Albert's flat into a bed-sitting room. I found one, a few streets away.

The house was owned by a former Polish Army officer called Grynski. He pressed a time-switch on the landing and led me up to the top room where he had retreated and where I gave him a cheque for £10 – two weeks' rent in advance. The room had musty smell. There were things under glass. Bits and pieces of his past. The statue of an archangel, the photographs of Polish soldiers, and small cactus plants on the dresser. On the walls drawings of a provincial town by a river. He was a tall man with straight white hair brushed neatly back and false teeth.

'Would you like to go back?'

'Yes,' he said. 'But I don't think I shall be able. Not with this government.'

He was reluctant to speak for long. And I wondered what I had in common with people like him. Just as I wondered when I went in for coffee in the pastry shop by South Ken. tube

88

station and saw more Poles, entire families, with children and a priest.

I dialled Eltham 6613.

Again it was Walter who answered. (When did he go to work?) I told him that I had moved and gave him the address and the telephone number. Then I sat back and waited for Anna to ring.

Grynski had the one phone in the house and every bed-sitter had its own buzzer. I didn't know the other occupants. I saw their names outside the front door, a series of small name plates with a black button beside each one.

I didn't like staying in. I was driven out. By the smallness of the room, by the little domestic things of having to have a shilling for the gas, another shilling for the electricity. Sometimes I would lie on the bed for hours, smoking, thinking of Anna. And that it was hopeless. But I didn't want to go back to Carnbray and Emily. So I rang the number. And got Walter on the phone. I don't know what we talked about. I invented some reason for ringing up. About an hour later I rang up again. Again Walter. He suggested that we meet for lunch tomorrow at Lyons Corner House in Piccadilly.

During lunch he said. 'Anna always has men around her. But I trust her. She believes in hell. There's a young actor. He went away to the Continent and came back with a white silk blouse for Anna. I made her return it to him.'

And as he talked I remembered the night in Penzance. She was wearing a white silk blouse. She told me she got it from a friend who bought it for her from the Continent. I was getting confused. Who was deceiving who?

After lunch Walter suggested that we go to see *Hiroshima Mon Amour*. It was on in a cinema in Bayswater. We found it opposite Whiteleys. In the middle of a love scene, with both of them in the nude, Walter whispered.

'The girl reminds me of Anna.'

She didn't remind me of Anna at all.

When we came out it was dark. We went into the nearest restaurant and had some coffee. Perhaps it was because of the film that made Walter tell me that Anna in bed tore the sheets. It was an intimacy. I suspected he wanted something in return. I told him that Emily in bed made a sound like someone sawing quietly. She made it with her toes. But that didn't sound as intimate as what he told me. So I made up stories. Of all the different women I had known on my travels when I was away from Emily and the kids. I'm sure Walter didn't approve. He wasn't promiscuous. And in his eyes I found it necessary to make as if I was.

Back in the bed-sitter I chain-smoked and waited for Anna to ring. In moments of desperation I would phone. And get Walter. He must have thought I was lonely for he would ask if I wanted to go and see an art gallery, another film, have lunch. I felt like a fool. I was beginning to know more about Walter than about Anna.

I did see her on Sunday when I came to lunch. Did I only imagine that she had cooled towards me. The snatched kiss when we were finally alone, and the nervous 'We must be careful. I'll think of something.' I suppose it was this insecurity that did the most trouble. I didn't know where I was with her. Or was it that now I began to suspect all sorts of things.

Walter drove us to the Common after lunch. And while we were walking ahead and Anna played ball with the boy. He said.

'Joseph, I'm frightened. I don't know what it is. But I think I'm losing Anna.'

I didn't feel superior to Walter. Suddenly we were friends, if one can say that.

The bed-sitter was becoming claustrophobic. But after four days I was getting used to it. I sat for hours in the chair, chain-smoking ... with half a loaf of bread ... the small teapot ... the open package of Brooke Bond Tea ... the packs of Gauloises. When I got hungry I'd walk to South Ken. tube station and get on a No. 17 to Piccadilly. Get off at Shaftesbury Avenue and walk to the Nosh Bar and have a couple of salt beef sandwiches with a pickle.

'Hello,' said the man behind the counter. His neat grey waves glistened. 'I caught your act last week.'

'I wasn't here last week.'

'Aren't you an actor?'

'No,' I said.

I don't think he believed me.

I rang up Charles. He said he wasn't feeling well could I come and see him.

I took a taxi. The door was open. I went up the stairs. Charles was in bed wearing dark glasses. 'I'm not well,' he said. 'I got pissed yesterday. I had such a bad night. I went into a pub yesterday before lunch and there was this boy. We came back here. He took off his shirt. And there was this rope around his chest.'

Charles got out of bed, went to his dresser, and from the top drawer took out a length of rope around three feet. He gave the rope to me. Then went back into bed. It was an ordinary rope, the kind Emily uses to hang up her washing, except it had two separate knots in it.

'Imagine being so uncomplicated,' Charles said, 'at so young an age. That you get up in the morning and put that around you and go out.'

'Did he know who you were?'

'No. We were in this pub. I was talking to an actor. And this boy said to me: You don't want to have anything to do with a cunt like that. And we came away. He said he would ring – I don't think he will. I wish I had his number. I'd ring him.'

The small record-player was on the table by his bed. He put on Edith Piaf singing *Non, Je Ne Regrette Rien*. The phone rang.

'Could you answer and find out who it is.'

It was someone called Ron who said he was a lifesaver.

'Say I'm not in.'

The shaky voice quivered.

'You know a man's body is much more physically interesting than a woman's, from a painting point of view. It's much more interesting the way it's made. A woman is much too flabby. She's made wrongly.'

The shaky voice quivered the French words. Charles watched me hold the rope.

'Joseph, a cock is such a small thing to be a man with.'

'Have you ever had a woman?' I said.

'Once. It wasn't very satisfactory.'

I put the rope back on the dresser.

'Would you like me to go out and get you anything?'

'I would like some tea,' he said. 'Could you go to the dairy on the corner and get a pint of milk, and an *Evening Standard*.'

When I came back I showed Charles the report on the front page that said Edith Piaf was dead.

I boiled some water in the kettle on the gas stove in the kitchen and made the tea. Charles still wore the dark glasses and his hand shook when he held the cup. Suddenly he got up and left the room and went in the direction of his studio. When he came back he gave me a new black leather jacket.

'I don't want it,' he said. 'Try it on. Button it up. It suits you.'

I told him a bit about Anna and that I had to go back to my room as I was expecting a phone call.

'I know,' he said sadly. 'I know how it is.'

Five days had gone by since I came up to London and I had not been able to get together with Anna. But I had seen Walter for three of those days. I couldn't let it go on like this.

Grynski appeared at the door. He was in his dressing-gown. 'There's a lady asking for you on the telephone.'

I ran up the stairs to the phone.

'Joseph – something terrible has happened.'

'What,' I said out of breath.

'Walter has found your letter. I left my purse behind when I went out shopping this morning. Walter went through it. And found your letter. I tried to tell him that it wasn't the way he was thinking. But he doesn't believe me. He won't talk to me. He has sent the letter to Emily. He said if he ever sees you again he'll punch you in the face.'

'I'll ring him up and talk to Walter.'

'How can you talk to someone who says he'll hit you in the face?'

Silence.

'Where are you?'

'In the High Street. This is the first chance I had to get away to ring you.'

'I'll try and stop the letter. I'll phone down there and see if I can stop it.'

'Walter won't have anything to do with me. He's not speaking to me.'

'I'll try and get the letter stopped,' I said. 'If I can't, I'll go down there.'

But who was down there that I could phone. Only Jimmy. I rang him, told him briefly what happened. He said he would try. But I thought he was too much of an English public schoolboy to do anything illegal. I wasted a week's rent with Grynski. And caught the morning train from Paddington and got into Carnbray just before five. As soon as I saw Emily I knew that Jimmy had not been able to stop the letter.

'It's not what you think,' I said.

'She left her ear-rings behind. I was going to send them on to her. But when I read the letter the first thing I did was to take those ear-rings and throw them in the fireplace.'

'Nothing happened,' I said. And I didn't sound very convincing.

'I thought we could be friends,' Emily said. 'I liked her. When the letter came I saw the envelope had Eltham Park on it. I was so pleased. A letter from Anna. She said she would write. And then reading it. At first I thought it was a letter to me. Then that it was a joke. And she came back to kiss me.'

The children were now in the house. They wanted to know about London. I had come back without food or presents. They sensed something was not right. I went out for a walk. Down to the front, along the harbour rails, by the church, the ladies' lavatory, through narrow side streets, by the closed restaurants, the Guildhall, the real estate office, the Co-op. Six years ago there would have been half-a-dozen places I could have gone in.

I went to the bar of The Metropole. There was only the barman, in the corner, playing dominoes with a customer. I had a brandy. Above their heads a commercial calendar showed a smiling girl in the nude sitting on a swing. Under her legs, D.M. Harvey: 'We manufacture short tools.' I arranged to meet Jimmy.

'I couldn't stop the letter,' he said as soon as he came in. 'The postman said he couldn't give it to me. Are you in the doghouse?'

'Yes,' I said.

Next morning I went to the bank and there was a letter from Anna. She said she was sorry for what happened. But she was in a bad way. Walter wasn't talking to her. And she was beginning rehearsals. What happened in Carnbray? Was I able to get the letter stopped? Could I write and tell her everything?

93

To avoid detection I would have to write to a friend of hers, a married woman whose husband was a builder in Suffolk. She gave me the name, Mrs Shipjack, and an address in Wood-bridge. She said Mrs Shipjack would take my letter and put it in an envelope and address it to her – so that Walter wouldn't know.

I don't know whether it was Emily. Seeing her carrying the can for all this. But suddenly the whole thing went sour. All this deception, these dramatics, for what? I decided not to reply. Three days later another letter came from Anna asking me to let her know what was happening, via Mrs Shipjack. Walter wasn't talking to her. And life was awful.

I began to suspect that she left the purse behind on purpose so Walter could find it.

I had only another eight days to go before I left for my trip to Canada. And Emily had as little to do with me as possible. I stayed out of the house as much as I could. Or else I came up here and read the paper. When I saw Emily she didn't say any-thing, but her look was a reproach. At night we slept in the same bed but as far apart as we could.

On the sixth day that I was back I woke at around five and found myself right up against Emily and that I was very firm. She was asleep on her side with her back to me. I moistened a finger in my mouth and brought it to her groin and gently tou-ched her. I did this again. It was moist. I shifted my weight and entered her from behind. She continued to sleep. I began, slowly, to move inside her. And Emily, in sleep, began to push back. Perhaps it was no more than a response to an old habit.

In the morning when I came down for breakfast she said. 'Would you like an omelette?'

It was the first time she offered to make anything for me since I was back.

94

Chapter Twelve

I WAS returning to a country I find sad and, after a few weeks, feel isolated in. Yet watching Montreal in the snow appearing under the port wing, then on the walk to the airport building, tasting the cold air, then the drive in the taxi, seeing familiar frozen streets, gave me a kind of happiness.

I shaved in the washroom of Windsor Station. And left my bags. Then walked to Ben's and had a smoked-meat sandwich and coffee in an almost deserted barn of a restaurant (not like the old times in the small place across the road). And came back to Windsor Station (the doors still open without being touched) and got on the train.

The relaxed luxury of sitting in a heated air-conditioned coach, piped-in music playing softly 'There's a Small Hotel'. The seat tilts back and you move, in the warmth, through a frozen landscape, past the suburbs, and into the country.

The person beside me was French Canadian in his early twenties. He said his name was Howie and that he came from Hull. He said he was an ex-engineer and had been celebrating. He had just bought himself out. And didn't know what he was going to do. He liked the engineers but not the officers. 'They treat you as if you're nobody,' he said. 'I'd do anything – I'd even kill someone – so people would know of me.'

I said I knew how he felt.

'A man came to me last night and said you can have my wife for sixteen dollars all night. What do I want his wife for? I want a girl. Can I see your paper?'

I gave him *The Star*.

I left the seat and walked to the observation coach, up the narrow stairs, to the comfortable seat, the glass sides, the glass roof, and the gentle piped-in music. Every time I come back and see this fine machinery, the kind of luxury it gives, I expect it also to produce a different kind of human being to go with it.* Outside. White birches, washing on a line, crows flying low over a snow field.

---

*I thought of the other trains. With observation cars. And stew-

95

Approaching Ottawa by the frozen canal (where I went to school) the train began to slow down. Under the humped bridge (where I rode my blue c.c.m. bike) it stopped for signals. I left the train and entered Union Station and took a taxi from the side entrance. Passed the Post Office (where I would walk to send out letters on weekends or late at night). Along Rideau ... these stores, these streets. They have meant more to me than anywhere else I have lived. The taxi turned off Rideau and stopped opposite a frozen park.

It was a new building with a glass front and a drive-in. As I came through the glass doors I felt the heat. Men were standing in the lounge. I went to the reception desk. The man behind the desk was in his thirties but there was grey in his hair. He wore a lumberjack shirt that looked like a bad imitation Scotch plaid. On the desk a nameplate: J.O. Charbonneau.

'I have come to see Mrs Grand,' I said.

'Is she expecting you?'

'Tell her that her son is here.'

'Mr Grand.'

'Yes.'

'I'll see if she's in.' He hesitated. 'You have come from England?'

'Yes.'

The man behind the desk went through another set of glass doors and disappeared. And a thin man standing in the lounge, the only one dressed in a suit, came up.

'How was England?'

'It was raining when I left.'

'I know your mother. I have a great deal of respect for her.

---

ards in white jackets. You got hot soup and coffee, hot dogs and hamburgers. And music was piped in: This Way for the Gas, Ladies and Gentlemen. *At the station a band was playing. There were flags and people looked gay and excited. A pleasant woman's voice over the loudspeaker:* This Way for the Gas, Ladies and Gentlemen. *People went to the exit doors. They lined up at the taxi ranks outside. It was cold. Snow on the ground. A Salvation Army group was singing* Silent Night. *The air was crisp.* This Way for the Gas, Ladies and Gentlemen. *The black taxis filled up with people and drove away. Exhausts smoking in the cold air.*

How long will you be staying here?'

'A few days.'

'Then we'll see each other. I'm Wilson, on the fourth floor. Number 412. You can come and visit me. I used to be a judge. I'm also a Texas Colonel.' He took out his wallet. Dark eyes, a spaniel-like face, he spoke in a soft voice. From his wallet he took out a card that said he was a Colonel in the Texas Army. 'I was born in Dublin. Have you been to Dublin?'

'Yes,' I said.

'Do you know the Haughtons there?'

'No.'

I felt awkward. I had expected a different welcome. But then I didn't know what my mother's new place was like.

A plump woman with silvered hair and a powdered skin came through the locked glass doors and into the lounge then went outside in the cold. She had on a winter coat with a dark fur collar. And carried a toy dog inside her coat, only the small head with the large brown eyes showed.

'You may go Mr Grand,' Charbonneau said. 'Second floor.'

The locked glass door opened and I went to the elevator. Waiting for it, I read the sign on the notice board. 'Money for the wreath to be sent for Mrs Clark's funeral can be left at the desk. Signed J. O. Charbonneau.'

When the elevator stopped I turned the corner and there, at the end of the corridor, was my mother waiting by the open door of her apartment.

'Hello,' I said and kissed her.

'Hello dear,' she said. I could have been coming from a weekend in Montreal.

She had not changed much from the last time. The only sign of ill health was the paleness of her face and the light blonde hair had thinned and started in places to turn grey.

'This is very nice,' I said looking at the kitchen with the new fridge, the new electric stove, the new sink unit. The sitting-room with the carpet, the chesterfield, the plants by the window, I remembered from before.

'It's smaller than the house. But what do I need a large house now. Everything is here. There's no mess.'

Through the window I could see the black trees, the snow, of the park.

'It's called for Senior Citizens,' she said. 'I was lucky to get a place. They have a waiting list.' My mother always liked euphemisms. Senior Citizens was easier to take than people who were getting on and who didn't have much money.

'What's this?' she said.

'A leather jacket.'

I was wearing the black leather jacket Charles had given me.

'It don't look nice.'

Next day I was to find out what she meant. When I came back with her in the afternoon she introduced me to Charbonneau.

'Yes,' he said surly. 'We met.'

While she went to her mailbox, Charbonneau said to me: 'Charity begins at home.'

'What did he mean by that,' I asked her as we stood side by side going up in the elevator.

'It's my fault,' she said. 'I told him that the reason you were wearing the black jacket was because you gave your coat away to a poor man in England before you left.'

'But why did you say that?'

'I don't know. I let my tongue run away. I was hoping to make it better. But I made it worse.'

'It's a good jacket,' I said.

'I'll explain to him later.' She seemed upset.

'You don't have to explain.'

But whenever we walked through the hallway she kept on introducing me to the other Senior Citizens as 'This is Joseph Grand.' To her I was now a writer.

Outside I said. 'I'm your son. Why don't you introduce me as this is my son —' But as soon as I said it I wished I hadn't. What did she have left? The picture on the wall when I was nineteen, the Book of the Month Club selections between the glass unicorns, the scribblers from school in a drawer, and memories.

She said. 'How is Emily and the children?'

'Fine. They all send their love.' I brought out some children's drawings that they insisted my taking with me. And a small wooden dish shaped like a flower that I got in Penzance. 'This is for you.'

'You shouldn't have done this.' She put the dish in her glass enclosed cabinet where I saw, from previous visits, the Leach mugs, the large bowl, the bottle of brandy. Together with the fragile pyramid of good china that she rarely used. They stood opposite the dresser with the nickel-plated samovar, the silver candlesticks used every Friday night, the brass drinking cup once used for Elijah's cup at Pesach. When I see this – and the rubber plant, the drawers packed tight with Ashkenazi prayer books, my father's tallis – I know that once I belonged to something.

'Someone wanted to give me a hundred dollars for the samovar,' she said. 'I didn't want to sell it. We can go and see Dad tomorrow afternoon.'

'How is he?'

'You'll see. I tried to get off work today, but I couldn't. I've got tomorrow and the next two days. I'll cook you some of the things you like.' She disappeared into the kitchen while I went and washed.*

When I came out there was a place set for me at the table. She took out a platter of gefilte fish from the large fridge.

'I got the fridge when uncle died. He left me a little money.'

I ate hungrily. 'Delicious.' I have never tasted gefilte fish like hers. Nor salted cucumbers or lutkas.

'Why don't you eat?'

'I have to watch my weight and my diet. And when you're alone you don't feel like cooking. You look better than the last time.'

The last time. It was a Greek Line boat. It took nine days to cross the Atlantic. And the Greyhound bus took four hours from Montreal. Then a taxi from the bus depot. I ran, excitedly, into the house, said Hello, kissed them, and said I had a taxi outside. Could they let me have two dollars to pay the driver. They laughed. 'You haven't changed.'

'It's time I got dressed,' she said. 'I've made a new winter coat.' She took a fur coat off a wooden hanger. I helped her into it. It was black astrakhan. She looked like something out of Chekhov. 'I had a patient for five years. A very rich man. Then he died. He left me a little money. I got this coat.'

'It looks nice,' I said 'Expensive.'

And she did look distinguished. You would never have

---

*We don't talk much mother and me. We never have.

guessed by looking at her that she was going to the hospital to stay up all night. 'I can't stay at home by myself,' she said. 'I get lonesome.'

'What time do you get back?'

'Around seven in the morning. There are things in the fridge. There's TV and *The Journal*. Goodbye dear.'

It was after I closed the door of her apartment that I saw the piece of cardboard in the metal holder by the door. 'In case of emergency call Doctor Stillgoe' and a telephone number. And below that, 'Rabbi Burns,' and another telephone number. It came with the new stove, the new sink unit, the view of the frozen park that once was a cemetery.

I felt tired but unable to sleep. The time was 7 p.m. Midnight in England. Emily and the children would be asleep. I put on the black leather jacket, the warm gloves, walked to the Canadian National on Sparks Street and sent Emily a cable. Then walked through the deserted snow streets of Lower Town with their winter double doors and double windows. I had come out of these streets. But I was condemned to want other things. On Murray Street, in front of the house where I had grown up, I saw a kid playing with a hockey stick and puck on the hard-packed road underneath the street light. His goal posts were small mounds of snow. And he was going through an imaginary defence. I watched him with nostalgia.

I didn't hear her get back in the morning but when I woke up it was after ten and she was already up and had breakfast waiting for me on the table.

'Did you sleep well dear?'

She had taken her plants out of the room where I slept. And now began to bring them back to their places by the window. The room was full of dried air. My toothbrush was stiff, the bristles felt like chalk. I was wearing a light shirt but I felt warm. Outside it looked like an old-fashioned Christmas card glittering with frost.

After breakfast she placed an electric razor, a banana, and some cream crackers in a bag. I got the taxi to stop in the market, bought some dahlias and roses from a farmer's stand. Then told the driver to go to the nursing home.

'How is Mona and Oscar?'

'She's got her own troubles. Oscar has to go out shooting

crows. She says they come too near their house. She thinks they bring bad luck.'

The nursing home was in the west, the far side of Ottawa. Nursing Home turned out to be another euphemism. It was a place for incurables.

'Good day Mrs Grand.'

'They all know me,' mother said as we walked along the long corridor with the marble floor, the rooms on both sides, the smell of hospitals, and passing nurses.

She entered a room. I saw a man in a wheelchair by a bed. His face was lying on the bed. I thought this must be my father. But it wasn't.

He was to the right sitting in a chair that had a canvas band across so he wouldn't fall forward. He looked small and frail.

'Hello Paw,' I said and squeezed his hand.

'It's your son,' she said.

His mouth opened. His face creased as if he was going to grin, tears appeared. But no sound.

'It's your son,' she said.

He looked at me again, opened his mouth, and said nothing.

'Do you know who this is?' She insisted. 'Do you recognize your son?'

'What kind of a question is that,' he spoke slowly and with difficulty. The tongue seemed too large for his mouth. Then his eyes left us.

'He's off in his world again,' she said. She often spoke of him as if he wasn't there.

'Do you think he recognized you?'

'I think so.'

'I don't know,' she said.

She broke a cracker and left it on the side of his chair. He reached over and I saw how delicate his hands were as he brought a piece of cracker to his mouth. He chewed it a long time. Then she peeled the banana, broke it for him into small pieces. He took a piece and put that into his mouth.

'That's all he's interested in – food. If I didn't peel the banana he would try to eat it with the skin. *How do you like these flowers? Joseph brought them.* Once some flowers were left too close to him. He began to eat the flowers.'

She wheeled him out, down the corridor, into a large empty room that had the far wall all glass and we could see the snow, the dark trees, the sky, and the frozen river.

A nurse in glasses came in. I was introduced to her, Miss Hébert. She was French Canadian. 'Are you his son?'

'Yes,' I said. 'How is he?'

'He's our favourite.' She spoke as if we were all deaf. 'We call him Mosey.' She bent over him. 'We dressed him up last week. *Eh Mosey?* Put on a clean white shirt and a black tie. We had some pillows. Sat him up. We made a paper crown. Put it on his head. He was King. *Eh Mosey? You like that. You like being King?*'

My father grinned. I don't think he understood what she was saying. I felt near despair. And I was getting off easy.

Miss Hébert left. Mother told him that I walked to the old house on Murray Street and the small tree that he had planted in the front garden was now higher than the house.

'From big things,' he said slowly, 'little things come.'

'He's got it upside down,' she said. But you could see she was pleased. 'He says a lot of things like that – back to front.'

She shaved him with the electric razor. And he sat in the chair, not moving, looking out of the plate glass wall. If one of us touched his arm, he looked at us. And if we asked him a question he opened his mouth and got a bit red in the face. Then he would leave us and return to stare at the winter scene outside.

A sudden noise from his throat. We both looked anxiously. Then I saw he was watching a grey squirrel, on the branch of a tree, undulating its bushy tail.

'Anything the matter,' a young nurse asked.

'No,' I said, 'just old age.' And as soon as I said it I wished I hadn't. It was easy to be cynical, to be smart.

We left him in his own room, staring at the door. The other man in the wheelchair still had his face lying on the bed.

'He's never talked so much before,' mother said as soon as we were outside.

I thought it would have been better if he had died before this happened to him.

'I would rather have him like this than not at all,' she said.

Next day I was interviewed by journalists. In England I'm just a travel writer who appears in women's fashion magazines. And if I'm noticed at all it's for 'the cleanness of the prose'. Probably because I had to learn English as a foreign language. I have a small vocabulary. No long words. But here I'm a bit more. In the hunt for Canadian Literature even travel writers are collected, made a bit of a fuss of. I was going to meet a lecturer in English in the lounge of the Chateau Laurier. It was mild. I decided to walk. Icicles hung from the edges and every so often there is a flash of white, a noise, as an icicle falls into the snow. He was going to write an article about my work for a little magazine. I already knew the pretentious phrases. The way the piece would be slanted. A Canadian in England would become 'an expatriate' and linked to the American expatriates of the 1920s. And since I wasn't successful, not yet, I would be someone worth writing about in the little magazine. While the larger periodicals won't touch you until you have made a lot of money. He was very neat, very correct. I suddenly felt a little envious of him. He was a Canadian of three generations. He was older than the country. We didn't have much in common. 'Mr Grand. Do you come for a renewal of roots?' He was, he looked, firmly rooted here. But at the same time it produced this shallow looking individual, provincial, innocent. 'Why do so many of our writers live out of Canada,' he asked. 'I don't know,' I said. 'People leave for personal reasons.'

I also kept bumping into people I had grown up with. Rudy Marks,* who had fish and butcher shops in the market and liked to gamble, called from the telephone in his car. He wanted to know if I could go and play pool with him at the Curling Club. 'You're the only one I know who won't be working at this time of day.' How did he know I was back? But then I was to find out that mother had telephoned *The Citizen* and *The Journal*. And there was a small notice in the social column, below the Queen and the Duke of Edinburgh – what they were doing in England – and the Governor General in Quebec. We played pool for twenty-five cents a game and drank gin and tonic and talked about people we once knew. 'You remember Chief.' 'Chief?' 'Yes, Chief, he played ball with us. He's dead. And Phil Croll, he died in the street, heart attack. Do you know what happened to Syd and Dolly –

When we were sixteen and seventeen we hitch-hiked regularly on weekends to Montreal, Toronto.

they're divorced. And little Peewee – he's a knocker. He puts up big apartment blocks. And Matthews died. Remember how he taught us to spell arithmetic?' 'A Red Indian thought he might eat tobacco in church.' Rudy talked as he played, sometimes to himself, 'Oh Marks, you fool you –' when he missed a shot. 'Remember the Français?' (For a dime on Saturdays I saw Tom Mix, Ken Maynard, Bob Steele.) 'When they pulled it down I bought one of the seats. I've got it installed in my den.' He showed it to me when we went back to his all white house. He had his name outside the door in wrought iron. His initials on his car, on his shirt, on his cuffs. And inside, surrounded by all the latest furniture and gadgets and lighting, a shabby moth-eaten, green cinema chair.

He said his wife left him and took their young boy. 'She used to try to undermine my confidence. We have all these things. You name a new gadget – we've got it. But you know she'd spend her time filling in coupons to get *free* samples. Tubes of cream, scent in a bottle, free breakfast foods ... As if she couldn't afford to buy them. Then she tells me she is bored. And wants to do something. Next day she says she's got a job going to doors and asking how many cups of coffee they have for breakfast? She was insulting me. I began to stay out late. And when I came home we would fight.'

I told him a few vague things about Emily, the kids, Carnbray, writing, the kind of life we lived.

'Those that have steady jobs,' he said, 'they win all the time. Maybe it's right that they should.'

'They don't win at everything,' I said.

We continued to play pool and drink gin and tonic while the light outside faded and the snow on the ground had some blue in it.

Later in the evening an Army Major appeared at the door of the apartment. He looked like a boy scout leader. 'I bet you don't know me,' he said. And I didn't at first. It was Buck Jones. We both went to York Street school. He had a white pony then and sometimes rode it to school. He said he was the recruiting officer for this district and drove me to his mess on the outskirts for a drink.

'This is a good country,' he said. 'You ought to be here. You're one of us.'

Am I, I wondered.

He parked the car and we got out into the cold and walked across the flat perimeter with the banked snow glistening on either side.

I couldn't fit in. I belong to a Parliament Hill that didn't have the changing of the guard, to a Sparks Street that was full of traffic, to a King Edward Avenue when it was a boulevard of tall elms.

'I can't hear you,' the Major said.

'I didn't say anything.'

'My hearing aid is frozen.'

In the mess we had a drink while we waited for the hearing aid to defrost.

'I saw Rudy Marks earlier today,' I said loudly. 'We played a few games of pool.'

'*Him.*' The recruiting officer had his face close to my mouth. 'He has bad breath.' And I moved my face back. He saw someone across the room and excused himself. While he was away I listened to two young Lieutenants talk about the west coast as the best place to go and live when they get their pension. Then a Captain, his hair cut almost to his scalp, came up and introduced himself as 'Al Magazine'. I told him my name. He asked if I was a Canadian. I said I was. Perhaps my name sounded to him as unreal as his own. 'Are you related to the Grands in Saskatoon?' 'No,' I said. The recruiting officer came back. 'I'm sorry about that but I have a sideline. I sell insurance. Will you have the same again?'

It was very pleasant over the next few days. I felt free, for a while, of all the things I left behind. And I like winter. I like the snow, the frost, the crisp air. And I was liked because I was not staying. I wasn't a threat to anyone. Just a warning.

But after a week it was time to move on. I told mother I'd be back before returning to England. And next morning, on the train to Montreal, passing through the suburbs ... the neat white streets, the comfortable wooden houses with blue roofs, icicles on the sides, snow on the lawns ... I had run away from this,*

---

*I remember the early travel articles about Canada that I wrote in England. I wrote about the violence, the mediocrity of the people, the provincialism, the dullness ... And all the time I wanted to be there.

yet I found I envied the man who lived here. The steady job, the regular income, kids going to the schools one went to. One could have a stake here. Pure Spring, Esso. Player's Please. And the steeple of a church rising above the houses and the buildings. MacDonald's Export. The train increased its speed and gave that smooth hum of a whistle like the bass part of a mouth organ. Passed empty fields with trucks abandoned in the snow. The glare from the snow. Washing hanging out. The long winter underwear. Then by an open crossing with the red arm flashing in and out like a heartbeat, the cars waiting on either side. Why can't I settle for this? Why isolate myself in a cut-off seaside town in England, that I don't even like?

And I wished I knew the answer.

Chapter Thirteen

I ARRIVED back in Montreal at noon, walked down St Catherine and took a room in a small hotel above a tavern at St Lawrence where nearly everyone spoke French, where the restaurants were Chinese, and the small stores had permanent Sale signs painted in white across the windows. The room was looked after by Monique, a plump Frenchwoman in her fifties and run by Lucien, equally stout, a crew-cut of grey hair and wearing a bow tie. Lucien said fifteen dollars a week. I said twelve. He said thirteen. I said all right. The room was new and clean but the noise from St Catherine went through it as if there was nothing to keep it out. Outside the window a car-park and over it a green neon with a turning globe advertising Woodhouse's furniture store. I lay down on the bed and slept for three hours. Then got up, washed, and went out.

I like being back in Montreal. I walk around seeing what has remained the same, what changes. I go to all the restaurants I know: Pauzes for oysters, smoked-meat sandwiches at Ben's and Dunn's, steaks and frankfurters and pickles at The Steak House. I spend a lot of time in the Honey Dews having cups of coffee, reading *The Star* and *The Gazette* (they were full of cemetery plot scandals) and listening to the old tunes (just music, no words) being piped in. At night I hear the sirens of a police car, an ambulance, a fire engine. Next day I read in the papers that there were six hold-ups, two shootings, and half-a-dozen fires. They are listed in a box, daily, like a weather report. I like this kind of life. I like being taken out of myself. I like the visible world. And I like to record what's going on around me.

I spent the first ten days walking through the streets. Winter was still here, mainly in the side streets. Pools of melting snow froze at night locking discarded newspapers, cigarette packs. Then released them in the morning. I walked around the mountain (very still except for the squawk of a peacock), the length of Sherbrooke and St Catherine, down through the docks, through the Jewish section. Noting things down. I write down the signs. The woman's barber shop with prices in Greek. The handmade signs in the stores: 'Send parcels behind

the Iron Curtain – two years to pay.' The billboard signs standing on stilts, DIEU EST NOTRE PERE. I cut things out of the
newspapers.

1410 on your dial
Serious and sincere your bilingual host
Hubert Langlois on the air Monday to
Friday. If you like good music – listen

SATURDAY		SUNDAY	
9 am	Back to the Bible.	8:00	Mass in Italian.
9:30	Greek programme.	8:30	Italian programme.
1:00	Ukrainian programme.	12:00	Jewish programme.
2:00	Polish programme.	2:00	German programme.
4:00	Spanish programme.	6:00	Italian programme.
6:00	Italian programme.	9:00	Greek programme.
8:30	German programme.	10:00	Dutch programme.
9:30	Irish programme.	10:30	Hungarian programme.

I turned on the radio. Someone on the Sacred Heart Hour
was giving 'inspirational messages'. On another station, a rich
man was opening a poor section. I jot down the pet shop with
the baby chicks dyed green, blue, purple, red. The Ferris wheel
turning in the window of the music store with the Viennese
waltzes coming out from a loudspeaker. In a new undertaker's
window, on Park Avenue, letters to the owner expressing sat-
isfaction for the sympathy that was shown. They all began:
'Dear Mort'. People don't seem to mind walking along the
street with labels pinned on them* giving their name and
address.

All this trivial material that I was gathering I find necessary. It's only later, in Carnbray, that I'll read over these notes
and see a pattern. And from them do the articles. Then something happened.

Perhaps it was because we were living cut off in Carnbray.
But after all this walking and looking I was tiring and losing

---

*I remember Emily, in Carnbray, saying: There are times I want to
go out of here with a badge that has written on it. 'Will you be my
friend'.

interest. And I suddenly didn't like what I was doing.

I wanted to bring some shirts to the laundry. Monique told me the Parkview Laundry was good. I couldn't find it. I stopped an old man with a cane walking ahead of me on St Catherine and asked him. He began to wipe his hand across his face, looked one way then the other, blushed, and said: 'I haven't been very well, my head, I'm a bit mixed up.' And later, there was this young woman with a child in a pushchair. She had large white cardboard cards and on them were words done in black paint. 'The snow is white, Robert,' she said loudly to the child then held up a card that said *The snow is white, Robert.* She went along a bit further and said: 'This is a street, Robert.' And held up a card saying *This is a street, Robert.* But the child had both hands on his face, his head was on a side as if he wanted to sleep. I followed her off Sherbrooke and saw her go to the door of a house. 'This is your house, Robert.' And as she opened the door there was a large sign inside saying *This is your house, Robert.*

I didn't like myself then. I was becoming ashamed of being an observer of human unhappiness. I remember getting Emily to come upstairs in the afternoon. After we undressed and got into bed and I had moved on top of her I said: 'Why do you close your eyes and put your hand over your face?' 'It's the light,' she said. 'I can see your face. I think this is just something else that you come with your notebook to look at.'

I had two airletters from Emily. I sent her and the kids picture postcards of Montreal. And wondered about Anna.

After two weeks in Montreal I left for Quebec City. And took a room in a cheap hotel in the student quarter, where the wood around the windows was painted a different colour from the rest of the house, as if to give them outlines. The seediness of Lower Town I knew from before. But it was the white grey stone that now dominated. It had the slowness, the dignity, of an old university town. but there was a deadness, a coldness about it all. A kind of boredom that one sometimes needs, of contracting out of life for a while. I thought Quebec City would be an excellent place to write a book. On my third day I went out to get a paper and felt my legs going, the street began to tilt. I never felt this way before. I wasn't drunk. I found I had to lean against the nearest house and sat on the steps. Then I made myself walk back to the hotel room, got undressed, and into bed. The room was pitching. I was afraid to close my eyes, when I did everything turned even more. I thought, how awkward it will be if I die here.

I don't remember when the knock came at the door but a small lady with glasses opened it. 'I haven't heard you type. Is there anything wrong. I always hear you type. I'm next door. You look like you have fever. Have you had anything to eat?'

'I'm not hungry. The room keeps going round.'

'When did you last eat?'

She brought me some chicken soup and crackers and grapes. And told me she was a writer too, Miss Ketchum. 'I taught school, then I had a car accident. It left me with my voice. It's much better now, but it hasn't come right yet.' She was going from coast to coast writing Canadian history for children. 'They don't want history taught like they do in history books. They're so dull. I know what children enjoy.' She told me she had gone across the country with her box camera, took photographs of statues, of rivers, of bridges, buildings, houses. And wrote a historical piece about them that she brushed up in the local library or museum or archives.

'I've done all the provinces, even Newfoundland. Quebec is the last.'

'What are you going to do after you finish?'

'I don't know.'

She came into the room, over the next two days, bringing more hot soup, chicken, grapes. 'It's wrong for you being away from your wife and children.' She showed me the complete manuscripts of Nova Scotia, Prince Edward Island, British Columbia, Manitoba, New Brunswick, all very neat, with her photographs pasted in. But no one wanted her books. Neither publishers nor education authorities. 'They all send the manuscripts back.' Yet she went on. She had her pension, she had some stocks and bonds. She sold her house. She had her car and she travelled. She carried with her a background of blackboards and chalk and children asking permission to leave the room. I hope we all have secret lives.

When I felt better she took me in her car to an old white house that was now a private hotel overlooking the frozen river. We went there to have tea and to watch the sunset over the snow and ice. There were two residents in the hotel. Two sisters, both widows, in their late eighties. They sat by the table next to ours. They also came to watch the sun. And they had the same conversation every time we were there.

'Did you see Jenny, it's going down.'

'Yes. I see it.'

'Don't let's look for a minute.'

'No, I won't look.'

'It's nearly down Jenny, it's going down.'

'I can see it.'

'Don't let's look for a minute.'

'Can you see it?'

'No.'

'It's down now.'

'Yes, it's down.'

'Draw the curtain. We'll go to bed.'

'I'll go first, Jenny.'

'I'll follow presently.'

On Sunday night I returned to Montreal to the room in the small hotel above the tavern. And on Monday morning I walked to the paper shop by the corner of Guy and St Catherine and I bought all the airmail editions of the British papers I could get. 'An outstanding new talent.' 'A sheer delight.' 'I'm not much of a gambler these days but I would like to put a bob on Anna Likely —' I didn't expect this. But it didn't surprise me. There were pictures of Anna – not the way I remembered. And I wondered if she was still having a silence period from Walter.

That night I picked up a girl in the lounge of the Mount Royal.

'Would you like a drink?'

'Thanks,' she said.

She was pretty with a large bosom, a small waist, tall, short blonde hair, and very nice eyes. She couldn't have been twenty.

'I'm much older than I look,' she said, guessing my thoughts. 'I'm twenty-three.'

She told me her name was Louise, that she came from New Brunswick. And that she worked in a library.

'What is your work?'

'Waiter,' I said. And as soon as I said it I wished I hadn't. I was being smart and there was no need. Waiter was what the income tax people put down as my occupation when they last sent me a tax demand. I saw this disappointed her. I guess she thought I was better than that.

'Where do you work?'

'In England,' I said.

'On holiday?'

'Yes.'

This seemed to make it good again.

'I've got a flat on Stanley,' she said. 'If you'd like to come back.'

We went back and it was no good. I don't know if it was Anna or Emily that hung over me like a conscience. I told her that I promised a woman I loved that I wouldn't do it with anyone else. And left her a five dollar bill so that she wouldn't feel too bad about it.

Chapter Fourteen

IN CARNBRAY I'm a cautious man. At night I double-check to see if I have closed the lights in the rooms, that the gas taps are turned off the kitchen stove. I slide the bolt across the front and back doors. I take the plug out of the television and the electric fires. I check the windows, shut them and lock them. I keep track of Emily's periods. I have a Boots Scribbling Diary and running through it I have these entries. *E's (.) due.* Four days later: *Enter E.* Fourteen days from the start: *Height of C.* Another fourteen days: *E's (.) due.* Emily sometimes asks me. 'I've got the curse, am I early?' And I come up here and look it up. I keep a copy of business letters I send out and those that come in. I keep a record of bills, receipts. Every Saturday morning I type out a new list of where I have things out, being considered, and what payments I expect to come in. I note down how many typewritten pages I do in the morning, how many in the afternoon.

But as soon as I leave Emily and the children all this caution goes. In Quebec City I forgot about a kettle of water I had on the electric stove. It boiled dry and burnt out holes in the bottom. When I picked it up the molten metal dripped on the floor and burnt the linoleum. It didn't bother me at all. In London, at Albert's, after a couple of exhausting days and late nights – where besides seeing people and talking I eat rich foods, drink champagne – I come back and lie all next day on the couch unable to do anything except get up to be sick in the lavatory.

Emily and the children in Carnbray are my base. Without planning it, it has worked out that the only way of keeping something one values intact one needs to be isolated, cut off. (Or is it love that has made me like this?) I have seen too many people I've known separated or divorced. And when I married, I married for life. As I began to realize, sometimes with despair. Apart from the writing, it is the only thing I've got. And to keep it, caution has made me keep it isolated. What an admission. That the only way to hold onto things that matter is to opt out of society. Yet for all the value I place on keeping what I have in Carnbray I cannot take too long living the way we are. I must, after a while, run away from it. Even if it is only for those few days in London, or those few weeks in Canada. Is this something in oneself? Part of me wants the conventional and some other part wants to be outside society. Yet I cannot take one without longing for the other. And so the only way seems to be to live these separate lives.

When people in Montreal ask me: 'Why don't you live here?' What can I tell them. That I can't live here because my wife refuses to live here. I have left her and the kids behind as hostages, to make sure I return to Carnbray. (I don't tell them that they are also hostages for the overdraft at the bank ... the unpaid bills.) Or was another reason why I don't live in Canada because I didn't want to become a *Canadian* Jew. I couldn't make the change from what my parents were to what I see walking in Montreal and Ottawa. When it was necessary, at the start, to change one's name, to live with two calendars, and tell little lies about oneself – I told whoppers. (Maybe it was just a way of keeping something intact.) It was Emily, and living in England, that made me see that it was unnecessary to pretend to a bogus personality. I know one person in Montreal who has made the change with a certain style. His name is Lincoln Scott. I met him walking along St Catherine. I knew him before the war. When he and his father lived in Ottawa. In the early 1940s they moved to Montreal. Lincoln Scott is tall, dark straight hair. He looks a bit like Cary Grant. He drove me to where he lived on the side of the mountain. Lincoln Scott has a phoney name and lives in a phoney house with phoney paintings on the walls. But there is a nice feeling about him. He laughs at it all. He made his money out of textiles during the war. And he told me about having to keep two safes, two sets of books. 'This is sometimes called the B.M. Drive.'

'Bank of Montreal?'

'No,' he said, 'Black Market.'

Afterwards he drove me to St Catherine near Guy to a flat next to a tobacconist where his father lived. He introduced me to his father, a neat little man called Mr Shantz. I hadn't seen him for over twenty-five years. He reminded me of a gentle Mr Magoo. Nice spoken, very quiet, small man, glasses. He wore a handstitched suit, white shirt, woollen tie.

'I didn't recognize you,' he said. 'That means you'll be rich. What would you like to drink? I have some Napoleon brandy.'

He poured with a slightly shaky hand.

Shantz lived away from Lincoln Scott, in this flat with the rooms untidy, full of girlie magazines, newspapers, nude women in various poses, continental movie magazines with nude stills, and a large television set.

I told the old man that I was over here for a short while and that I was going back to England.

'I don't expect we'll see each other again,' he said. 'Live a hundred and twenty years.'

As we were walking along St Catherine Lincoln said. 'I don't understand him. My own father and he refuses to live with me. He goes off on these boat-cruises. And meets Jewish widows, divorcees, on board. Mainly Americans. They send him photographs, letters. I don't know what he can do, at his age, except give a little cough. He's over eighty. But he won't live with me. He likes his small flat, the mess it's in. Women keep dropping in to see him all the time. He must be very generous. He says they do things for him. Anything he wants.'

Chapter Fifteen

BACK IN OTTAWA to say goodbye. And driving in from Uplands it's no longer the way it used to be. 'I hope I'll still be here next time you come, dear,' mother said. Then steadied herself. 'I'm sorry. I don't usually cry. I don't know what came over me.'

At the nursing home. Father was alone in the room with the large plate glass window. He was watching broken hunks of ice being carried by the river. I stood by his chair and watched the grey-white chunks of ice go quietly by. We didn't speak, just watched, as a large chunk appeared then moved by very slowly and disappeared. I have always been touched by the silent breaking up of winter. There's something inevitable and majestic as these large hunks of ice move slowly along on the flat water. The minutes passed. The ice passed. We said nothing. A sadness in the room. I told my father I was going back to England.

'England,' he said and his face creased and brightened. Then he went back to watch the ice. It was time to leave. I kissed him on the forehead.

'What's all this kissing for?' he said irritably.

Whenever I return to England from Canada I'm struck how civilized England looks. And how shabby and drab the externals of that civilization are. Perhaps that is part of its appeal. I walked along Shaftesbury Avenue to the store with its windows filled by bottles. And bought a bottle of champagne. Then caught the 12:30 from Paddington. Up until Plymouth it's all right. After the snow and the slush, it looks very green. But after Plymouth the train begins to slow down, to stop at every station. And you feel you are going further and further into a backwater. A garbage dump. And once in Carnbray – the sea, the empty sand – and instant depression. And I wonder why the hell am I living here.

After kissing Emily I went upstairs. The kids, in bed, were not asleep. They all looked so handsome and excited. I showed them some of the things I brought back for them and that mother bought, dresses and things. Then went downstairs.

Emily lost weight. We had champagne and tried to give the kids a chance to fall asleep before we went up the stairs to bed. We were both anxious. And going into her, it felt as it used to after she had a period.

Next day, with the children off to school, we went back upstairs. This time some of the nervousness had gone. But there was still the strangeness. I discovered she had all sorts of little devices that I didn't know she had. And I wondered what books she had been reading. She scratched her nails on the side of my legs and groin. She also seemed to squeeze harder when I was inside. Perhaps I detected these unfamiliarities because I had been away or because Anna had passed by. Next morning when I went to the toilet, a satisfied exhausted feeling, the skin of the cock is smooth because of last night, the falling urine sparkled as the sun caught it, and the smell reminded me of French Canadian pea soup.

For the next week or so we were at it. We could now begin slowly and make it last. Sometimes we approached each other with words.

'Why are you so carnal?' she said.

'Because I've just promoted myself.'

When she had a cold or wasn't feeling well, 'I feel all blocked up.' For some reason this made me randy. And I would say, 'Have Dr Grand's cure.'

'You think this is a cure for everything.'

It was over quickly. We would raise a sweat. Then tired both fall asleep. And she did feel better next morning. So that when she felt a cold coming she said. 'I know. I'm going to get Dr Grand's treatment tonight.'

Sometimes when I came downstairs during the day and she was in a room. I went and lifted her skirt and put my hand between her legs. 'You know what's there,' she said.

'Come upstairs.'

'Rebecca will be back from school in fifteen minutes. Wait until tonight.'

Sometimes there were a few signs. Like that of giving me the core of an apple to eat. It began when we were hard up and I pretended I didn't want any apples. For all we could afford was a pound of apples. And after the kids and Emily had one – there were usually four – I didn't. Then Emily said, 'have the core'. I had the core. Later, when she had to teach and didn't want to fuck at night – when she ate an apple, she didn't give me the core. But threw it deliberately in the fireplace. When she did want to – she would give me the core. So it has become an intimate exchange, just giving the core of an apple she has eaten. I take it and I eat it. And going to bed that night has started with this.

Sometimes we have an unexpected visitor, a woman. And that was enough to get Emily up the stairs after the woman went. She would go with a token show of reluctance. 'I bet no one else can do it in the daytime, unless they have secretaries.'

Another time I came downstairs and before I could say anything, she said. 'I've got bad news for you. I'm leaking.'

Chapter Sixteen

FOR THE FIRST FEW WEEKS I can't take the way we live here. I've never seen it as shabby when I've come back from a London trip. I see how we only have one room where we are all in the evening, all around the coal fire. The television set is in the opposite corner. We must get a new chair. This one has the bottom falling out. But we don't get a new chair. Because this house isn't ours. This furniture isn't. I've picked up a few things, so has Emily. But there is always the constant reminder from Emily, from the children, that nothing here is ours.

'Is the table ours,' Martha asked.

'Yes,' Emily said.

'Is the television set?' Ella said.

'Yes.'

'Is the telephone?' Rebecca said.

'No, the telephone isn't.'

'How about the plates?'

'Some of them are ours.'

'The mattress —'

'My mattress is ours.'

'What else is ours?'

So I have this distance: between the house, the rooms. I even have a distance from Carnbray. I notice the apathy of the people here, their slowness. I go through the streets – what a small place it is – and come out to the front or to one of the beaches, the bay. But I've seen it so many times before. I go on a bus to Penzance, across the moors, just to be reminded that I don't belong here. I put on my Canadian winter coat, just to let people know I don't belong here. I come back talking with an even more pronounced North American accent. I read three London papers a day, three on Sunday. I listen to the news on the radio, on TV. I have these two wrist watches on my desk. One is set at the time in Ottawa and Montreal, the other the time here. So that looking at the one set in Canada I can say – at this hour, at this place, certain things are happening. I make phone calls to London. Write letters. Anything to feel in touch.

This lasts for a while.

Then I begin to close up the distance. Between Emily in a matter of days. And between the children just as quickly. But I still try to keep a distance from the house. By doing all sorts of things like drinking gin and tonics, or whisky, or smoking the Canadian cigars dipped in rum that I brought back. But the Canadian cigars run out, I stop drinking. When I look at the watch with the time in Canada it is just to see if people there are awake or sleeping. And it soon feels as if I've never been away.

I put together all my trivial material that I recorded of my stay in Canada and wrote the two articles without undue pressure. Except that I was no longer interested in writing this sort of thing. And when I received the rest of the fee I paid our bills. That left £205 in the bank. It was very pleasant not to have the pressure of worrying about money, of being able to feel not let down if the postman went by, though I still look out for letters. It was pleasant to go with Emily, when the children were at school, out to a good meal, then upstairs to the bed.

Emily didn't speak of Anna but we both read in the *Daily Mail* that the production was going over to Broadway. Later, I read that Anna and Walter had separated. And Anna was going on to Hollywood to be in a film.

Chapter Seventeen

JIMMY'S COME BACK from a trip to America. We arranged to meet at 2:15 at the bar of The Metropole. He came in, exactly on time, looking very tanned and healthy, and we had a whisky.

'How was it?'

'It's a marvellous country,' he said. 'It really is. I began in Maine. The leaves were changing colours. I've never seen such colours. Then I drove down to Florida. Then Texas. And Mexico. The morning was like a Chagall painting. There was this large sun, the cocks were crowing, and I was running around nude in the house with this woman.'

'How long were you in Mexico?'

'A weekend. I drove from there across to the Pacific coast, up to Seattle, then back to New York. It's the most exciting country I've been in. Drink up. Let's go to the house. I brought back some bourbon.'

Driving back to his place he said, 'England gets smaller and smaller every time I come back to it. It's so depressing. I feel shut in.' The light yellow sand was below ... the blue of the bay. 'I get a feeling of openness over there. I like the Americans. They've got sparkle, colour, brashness, even hysteria. But I feel much more alive over there. I have a feeling I can do things there that I couldn't do here. And their language. I went into a small beat-up cafe to get a hot dog. The waitress at the canteen called out on the microphone: One red hot coming up. Marvellous. In Florida a man warned me about a woman: She's a phoney from Phoneyville.' He enjoyed that for he repeated it twice. 'The women had cars and clean underwear. And nothing much to do in the afternoon. We would drive to some motel* ... I brought a record back.' He disappeared in the house and put on Kenny Ball's *Midnight in Moscow*. We drank on the lawn

---

*When I introduced Charles to him – Jimmy invited us for dinner. Afterwards Charles said: 'All the women he's supposed to have had. He's so romantic. If he did have all those women he'd keep quiet about them. He's a country yokel.'

121

while the music came out from the open windows.

'I've been offered a research thing at the marine biology place in Florida. I think I'll take it.'

'When will you go?'

'In the spring.'

'What about Esther?'

'She likes this house – but she'll go. Anyway I think I'm getting too old for all this running around. I want some of the home comforts.' He smiled. 'I could settle down over there ... Drink up. I made £200 today from some shares.'

He filled the glasses again. *Midnight in Moscow* was repeated. A hot afternoon. The green of the trees, the ice-blue water flat in the bay, the pastel colours of the far shore fields, the long neat lawns, the all white timbered house ...

When I came back Emily said. 'How is Jimmy?'

'He's fine. He had a good time in America. I don't know why but every time I come back from his place – I have a good time there – but every time I come back I feel depressed and poor.'

Chapter Eighteen

THE PHONE RANG. It was Charles.

'Where are you?'

'I'm in London, having breakfast at Lyons. I thought of coming down for a few days. Could you get me a room in a hotel? I'll take the overnight train and come straight up. I'll tell you my news when I see you.'

Suddenly it's exciting. I ring The Riviera Hotel and fix him up with a room. I tell Emily when she comes back from shopping that Charles is coming. And there's excitement in the house. I don't know anyone who generates excitement like Charles.

Next morning we get out of bed early. I roll up the newspapers, chop some wood, and make the fire in the front room. And keep glancing out of the window. And there is Charles coming up the road. In that slow rolling walk of his. He is carrying a small overnight bag. He's got a grey flannel suit and a black rollneck sweater. And it's only 7:15 a.m.

He comes inside, kisses Emily and smiles.

'How was the trip?'

'Fine. I like trains.'

We have breakfast then go into the front room and he sits in the far chair. He sits in this way he has, on the edge of the chair, legs crossed, sideways, leaning forward, with one foot pointed up ... you can see it in his paintings as well.

'Have you been out of the country?'

'I went to Greece. It was all right. But not knowing the language doesn't help.

'We're still here,' Emily said. 'Like we were last time you were down.'

Emily brings in coffee. And he tells me of the literary people he has met. 'Iris Murdoch keeps on sending me postcards to meet her in an Earls Court pub. I spent a weekend with Henry Moore. He's got this lovely little Cézanne – it's the Cézanne I've always wanted.'

'How was Moore?'

'A sensitive man. He has that *grand* humility,' Charles said with a mischievous smile. 'Do you know Mary McCarthy?

She gave me an autographed copy of *The Group*.'

'What's it like?'

'As if the girls emptied out their handbags. What time is it?'

'It's 8:23,' I said.

'He always says that,' Emily said. 'Or it's sixteen minutes to one. As if time matters here.'

Then I walked him to the hotel. Suddenly life feels exciting. Emily also feels it. Even walking with him along the road feels different. We have a habit of leaving a sentence hanging midway as soon as one of us got the point. We would leave out words in our conversation simply because we could talk freely.

'We're lucky,' he said. 'To be able to live our lives this way. Take days off when we want.'

'After I finish a day's work I just want to go and see someone and talk. And there isn't anyone here.'

'I have this show in France in two months. I like the pictures better than any I've done.'

'Will you go?'

'I might. I was there last month. I was with this man in a pub having a drink. And he said let's go to Paris. So we went to Victoria and got on the Golden Arrow. It was marvellous doing it like that. There was a square. We sat in it. But he was a pederast. He only liked young boys.'

In the evening he came to take us out to the best restaurant in Carnbray. And of course he insisted on paying it all. He never lets you pay for anything. Once I insisted on paying for a round of drinks in a pub. 'But why,' he asked. 'It's only money.'

We walked him back to the hotel after the meal. By the front. A few lights from the French Crabbers in the bay. The green lights of the far shore fields. He seemed reluctant to go back to the hotel.

Next day he rang up just after one. 'I believe I'm supposed to come for lunch. But I had a terrible late night. I'm just getting up. Could I come in about half an hour?'

'Of course. How do you feel?'

'I got drunk last night – I had someone I met in the bar.'

'I thought someone had to do it to you.'

'I can do both.'

He turned up in about half an hour with a new lettuce and radishes and a cucumber in his hand. And Emily made a salad.

We know he likes salads. He saw Emily's cookery books on the white shelf in the corner. He picked up a paperback. 'Did you know she has lost her sense of taste.'

Afterwards we went for a walk. Up the slope to the large houses, with trees and lawns, most of them converted to guest houses, hotels. Very quiet, residential. It could be the expensive part of any provincial town. Except for the view of the bay ... the palm trees ...

'You can always come up to London. And you've got your work. But it must be hard on Emily.'

'It is,' I said. 'There's no one here she can talk to. I saw in the paper —'

'Where I'm supposed to have made all that money?'

'Sixty thousand pounds.'

'It's not true. All I get is between twelve to fifteen thousand. The rest goes for tax.'

From the large houses we walked along a country road, then through stiles, across farmers' fields, and we were on the moors. The sun was shining. The water in the bay was in two colours. Very blue where no clouds were in the sky. And a grey white where there were clouds. Around us: the bright yellow gorse, the wood anemones, the small green fields with stone fences.

'Why isn't everyone out here?' Charles said. 'It's so beautiful.'

When he is here it is best to let him do what he likes for I know he does not like to feel himself being taken over by anyone. We asked him to come tomorrow for lunch. He said he would. He also said he would ring tonight.

He didn't ring. We guessed he must have met someone and was out late. And he would ring or just come up next morning. Next morning I waited. And kept looking out of the window. No sign or telephone call. Emily said she would prepare a Russian salad. And I made out a cheque for five pounds and she went to the bank to cash it. Just after eleven I couldn't wait any longer. I phoned the hotel. Emily said.

'You don't think he could have left?'

'Of course not,' I said. 'I don't want to speak to Mr Crater,' I said on the telephone. 'But could you tell me if he's still in the hotel?'

'He's gone,' the receptionist said.

'When?'

'This morning.'

'Thank you.'

I hung up.

'He's gone,' I said to Emily. We were both silent.

Then I picked up the phone again. And dialled the same number.

'I just rang about Mr Crater. What time did he go?'

'About 8:30.'

'Did he go to London?'

'I don't know.'

'Was he there last night?'

'Yes, he was.'

'Any messages?'

'No. Only a book for Mr Grand.'

'Nothing else?'

'No.'

It was raining, not a hard rain but I knew it would go on like this for most of the day. I went to the hotel and picked up the book I lent him, *Vogue's Gallery*. Then came back by the bus stop, the lookout. It looked very pretty, the harbour, the piers, the front.

We had the Russian salad in silence.

'It's very nice,' I said.

Chapter Nineteen

I HEARD of Jimmy's accident over the radio, on the local news, at breakfast. He was going up to London. His car went into a lorry just outside Salisbury. I called up Esther. She didn't take it too seriously. He would be laid up for a while she said but out of hospital in two weeks. I went down to the front and sent him a Donald McGill card – *Who says these are not real?*

But he never got it. He died late that night from a blood clot.

The funeral was large and formal, in the parish church. The mayor of Carnbray came and all the other civic dignitaries and members of various organizations as well as some people from the marine biology place. The vicar didn't know Jimmy but he knew the Middletons. And he went on about what the Middletons meant for this part of the country. What they had done. And how Jimmy was now part of history. He was buried beside his parents and grandparents where, the vicar said, he belonged.

Chapter Twenty

PERHAPS I'm writing like this because I miss people. There is no one here I go and see. And no one here comes to see us. Apart from Emily, the only talk I have with people are those I meet casually in the street.

When I walk down to the front in the morning for my newspapers I sometimes see The Voice of Calcutta. He's a stoutish man with glasses and a little black moustache. He does the statistics here for various opinion polls in London. He told me that before the war he was in the East working for an English bank and doing amateur dramatics on the side. He had a spot on a local radio station commenting on current affairs and telling jokes. 'I'd listen to the overseas service of the B.B.C., take down their jokes, then broadcast them in Calcutta.' He is against the government, against the royal family, against people with money. 'Put out the red flag. Did you hear the students are getting the workers out. *The workers.* They're so conservative. They haven't got any guts themselves. Good for the students ... I'd shoot them all. Give me a machine gun. I'd shoot the royal family. All the upper classes. And the priests and the archbishops. The whole fucking lot of them. My father and mother were poor. Why should these bastards get away with it for so long. They won't get away with it much longer.' He saw a labourer across the road going off to work. He shouts to him: 'Hullo – just going off to play polo?' Or to a decorator. 'Are you off to see your yacht?'

He can't walk very fast. If he sees me in the street he says. 'What's your hurry? You're going to die anyway. So stop and have a laugh. Have you ever been to Gweek?'

'No,' I said.

'There was this fellah and he had this virgin on the ground. He wanted to get on with it. But she got cold feet and wanted to put it off as long as possible. So she asked him.

' "What's your name?"

' "Brown," he said.

' "Where do you come from?"

' "Birmingham," he said.

' "Do you have any brothers and sisters?"

128

' "One sister – Now," he said, "I'll ask you some questions. Where do you come from?"

' "*Gweek*." ' And he let out a shriek. Then laughed.

'Here's another. There was this Catholic priest with his arm in a sling across his chest and there were these two beatniks. One beatnik said:

' "What's wrong with him?"

' "He probably fell in the bath," the other said.

' "What's a bath?"

' "How should I know. I'm not a Roman Catholic." ' And he laughed again at his own joke. He grew up in the East End of London. But he hates London. He likes Carnbray. Once, I asked him. 'What do you do when you feel depressed?'

'I go in front of the mirror and laugh – laugh like anything. And I feel better.'

His wife is a small good looking woman. She paints landscapes by numbers. She has painted the jungle, birds, butterflies. One afternoon she came up to me in the street. 'Hello Joseph. I feel awful. It's the change of life. I feel really rotten.'

'How's Jerome?' I said.

'I can't get him to go out,' she said. 'He stays in all the time watching television.'

Whenever I see the Russian lady we stop and chat. She is a tall woman, now slightly bent with age. She wears a brown duffle coat with white gloves and a veil over her face. And walks with a stick. I first saw her on the front, surrounded by cats, calling Poosie, Poosie. Then giving them pieces of butter from her pocket. She wasn't very good in English. She was happier in French. 'I have the very English name,' she said in that guttural Russian accent, 'of Anderson.' I often saw her walking quickly along the deserted front, through the back streets, not too good on her legs, as if afraid to stop. Then go into a doorway, take out a small bottle, have a drink, and walk on. 'I'm sure people think I'm a drunkard. But it's medicine for my heart.' She said she knew Rasputin. And described a formal ball she went to as a young girl in Moscow. And as she spoke I imagined her at the ball with a fan and bare shoulders. Even now she is a handsome woman. But she is frightened.

'The Bolsheviks are after me,' she said.

'But you are safe in Carnbray. They won't come here.'

'They will find me,' she said.

When I go down the road I sometimes see the tall thin spinster lady with a bright face. Miss Edwards. On fine days she stands by her door. 'When are you coming in? You say you will but you never do.'

I went in. I was with Rebecca. Her house was clean and neat. There was a picture of Henry Irving on the wall. 'We're related,' she said. And some paintings that looked pre-Raphaelite. She kept wanting to give things away. Books. Fruit. Rebecca finally had an apple and I an old copy of *The Playboy of the Western World*.

On cold winter days she would come out of her house only half-dressed. I'd button her blouse, her coat, put her brooch on properly at the neck. 'What have you been doing?' 'I don't know,' she said. 'I can never remember what I've been doing.' Once when I was doing up the top button of her coat she said. 'I'd just as soon die as go on like this.'

I see Russell Beck, by chance, about once a year. He's in his late thirties, a Canadian, very rich. He inherited money from both sides of his family. He was trained as an architect at McGill but has never practised. He has a house on the moors. He is part of that first summer when I was with the Captains and the Majors and the Squadron Leaders. I thought of him then as being very articulate, intelligent, he liked to discuss ideas. Probably because of his Jesuit schooling in Montreal.

Now when I see him he is in a car. He drove me back to his place where a woman I hadn't seen before was reading a paperback novel in the sun. She didn't say a word. There was a smell of newly cut grass. The house had an open look. Of complete idleness. 'It's a year since I've done any work,' he said. I tell him about my trip to Canada. He is not very interested. He shows me his cock and the four chickens. Lovely birds. Cock all nice colours. He gets an egg and brings it back. It's still warm and we all touch it. He goes and pees by the fence.

'My brother in Montreal has just become a director of the St Lawrence Starch Company.'

A feeling of complete idleness about the place.

'Do you see much of your farmer neighbours?'

'They're not very sociable,' he said. 'Methodists. They don't approve. Anyway I'm living like a hermit.'

'When does the postman come?' I said.

'I don't know,' Russell Beck said. 'We're never up when he comes.'

'He comes about 10:30 in the morning,' she said.

There were outbuildings all locked up. 'It used to be my studio. But I haven't done any work for a year. Sorry I haven't got anything to drink. We had some people last night and all we've got are two empty bottles.'

He called out to her: 'Get some tea and cake.'

And she does without saying a word.

We have the tea and cake outside. I see a magpie, then another, very close. And the gorse lovely. All orange yellow. Very bright gorse.

'I've been to Ireland for a month,' he said. 'I've been up to London for a while. I went to Amsterdam for two weeks. I've been to Portugal ...'

His place was overgrown. Only a cock and four hens. Green fields were all around. The smell of newly cut grass.

'It's very nice here,' I said.

'Life goes by very slowly,' he said.

About twice a year we get a phone call from our former greengrocer, now retired. She is a widow and a bit deaf and she shouts down the phone. 'Are you still in the land of the living?'

'Yes,' I find myself shouting back.

She doesn't go out of the house because she has swollen ankles. She relies entirely on the phone.

'How is everyone?'

'We're all right,' I said. 'How are you?'

'I've got piles,' she shouted. 'I've asked Mr Stock. He says he's got piles. And his wife's got piles. It's too much sitting down.'

She tells me her grandson came on Sunday and took her out for a drive around Carnbray.

'Where did you go?'

'Oh, the road along the cliffs.'

'Wasn't it nice?'

'I like it better inside,' she said quietly.

And there is the short woman, her hair parted in the middle, very bright face, further down the road. When I first saw her I used to meet her coming back from an afternoon on the front, sitting on a bench. 'I had a lovely time,' she said. 'I met so many people. They all talked to me.' Now she doesn't go out much. On Sunday afternoon she sometimes waits for me to go by to the post office and gives me an air letter to put in the letter box for her son in South Africa. I think it must be my accent or hers, or perhaps because she can't hear very well. For we have these conversations.

'Mist again,' she said.

'I think I'll make it,' I said. 'The collection isn't until five.'

'It was so thick coming in. It was hard to see.'

'I'm sure the train doesn't leave the post office until five.'

'Well, we can't complain, we had a couple of good sunny days.'

Another time as she gave me a letter, I said: 'Have you got a Wallis?'

'No, we have a record-player but it's broken.'

'If you have a Wallis, a decent one ...'

'No, I haven't got one. I have this record-player.'

'If you have a decent one you could get a good price for it.'

'Now?'

'Yes, now. He's having a exhibition at the Tate this summer.'

In May the closed summer restaurants re-open. Roads are paved. Cottages and house are freshened up with paint. So are the harbour rails. The junk shops have new and more expensive junk in the windows. And racks of picture-postcards everywhere. Emily and I went out for a walk to see the place before the season wore it down. We were walking along the High Street. Past the fruit shops, the pubs, the cafés, the gas and electricity, and saw the tall Swedish owner of The Paradise. She was standing in the doorway of her restaurant, her head tilted up towards the sun. She leaves Carnbray at the end of September and lives the winter in Stockholm.

'You're like the birds – you two,' she said seeing us. 'You come with the spring.'

I can't tell her that we are the ones who have been here all the time. So we smile and say, 'Hello, Inga' and walk on.

Chapter Twenty-one

THE RINGING woke us all up. I went downstairs to the phone. It was Oscar speaking from Meridian with Mona listening on the extension. After asking how we all were (I was shivering, I told him it was 2 a.m. Saturday morning here) he said father had died. (I think he expected me to cry on the phone.) The funeral was on Sunday at 2 p.m. Could I come? I said I couldn't get out of here and up to London and fly across in time (even if I had the money for the ticket).

After that I didn't go back to sleep. I got dressed, had some coffee, went out and walked to the front.

I didn't remember often the man in the hospital. But I remembered other times. The live chicken that he held and moved over my head when I was a kid. (Now what was that for?) The blessing he gave me before going to the synagogue. Telling jokes at moments of tension ... when I had to go overseas and we were waiting for a taxi. Anxious that we didn't harm ourselves. 'Be careful with the scissors. Watch how you are pointing that knife.' The best times I had with him were when I helped him to peddle fruit in the summer. The tall red wagon with the white horse. We left the Market by William Street and faced the traffic from Rideau. Then, finally, crossed over with the wheels of the wagon getting caught in the street-car tracks. Into Nicholas. Past Bytown Museum that always seemed shut. Past the jail with its high, small greystone, walls. Up Laurier Bridge. The horse straining. And at the top – the Peace Tower, the Driveway, the railway tracks, the canal. And down the other side, the horse holding back the weight of the wagon, the leather harness cutting into his rump. Across Elgin and into our first street, Gloucester. The horse stopped. He rolled back the canvas cover. A quiet street. No one outside. Houses with green wooden verandahs. Trees. And the greystone convent. Somebody is practising the piano ... They were the happiest days of my childhood. I got to know him then. And all the time I was made to feel ashamed. Because this was being poor.

On Sunday I wanted to do something. I just couldn't let it go like that. I put on a clean white shirt, the grey suit, blue tie.

Emily and the kids just watched. I said I was going to Penzance.

There was no synagogue in or near Carnbray. But I remember reading in *The Cornishman* that Penzance once had a thriving Jewish community.

But there was no synagogue in Penzance. All that was left of that Jewish community was an old unused cemetery. I found it, up from the railway station, through an opening that led to an alley between two backs of houses. At the top, St John's barnlike Church-house. It was squeezed between the Church-house and the backs of a row of terraced houses.

From the outside you would never know it was a cemetery. All it was was an old green door, with a lock and bolt on it, set in a high granite wall that went right around. The granite was built above the green door to give it added height so no one could see over. Nor could you see around the wall that enclosed the sides. Someone had gone over the granite with plaster. But the plaster had cracked and peeled. It was now various shades of faded orange, yellow and grey.

I decided to go to the address of the caretaker that was painted in white on the green door. The house was in Mount Street, a black door, just down from a pub. I knocked.

The man who opened the door was in his shirt. I asked him if he was the caretaker.

'Yes,' he said. 'Would you like to see it?'

'If it's not too much trouble.'

He went back in and came out with the key. He unlocked the lock, drew the bolt, and opened the green door.

I wasn't prepared for the smallness. It was about the size of a courtyard, enclosed by these high walls. And on the inside the walls were even more pink and faded. A small path, a few stones. And there were the headstones. Some in metal, some broken, some pushed to stand awkward in the back. In Hebrew and in English letters. I made out Hart. It said the parents of Lemon Hart, the rum family.

I saw a large toadstool growing in the grass.

The caretaker said it was a lump of bread that was thrown over from the backs of the terraces. 'It was so bad when I first took on the job that I had to go to the police to ask them to stop throwing rubbish into it.'

There was a lilac tree in one corner in bloom. Otherwise the place was overgrown, the grass was long.

'Who pays you to look after it?'

'People in London,' he said. 'I get a cheque once a year. They don't ask questions. Nobody has been buried here for over fifty years. I don't think there are any Jews left in these parts.'

I said 'Yiskadal, V'Yiskadash, smay Rahboh' to myself. It was all I remembered. And I didn't want to stay here any more. I had come to this place because of something in the past. Now, I felt no more than a tourist.

We started to go out. But the green door wouldn't open.

'Boys must have seen us go in,' he said, 'and slid the bolt across.'

I tried to push. It wouldn't open. He went up the side to where the backs of the terraced houses were and called out: 'Mrs Thomas, Mrs Warren, Mrs Hope.' He tried again. 'They must be out.'

I tried to climb up the wall but fell back, there was no foothold. He called out 'Hello ... Hello ...' We waited. Nothing happened.

'We can't get out,' he said.

After that we didn't talk. We stood there listening. I heard gulls, jackdaws, a train shunting in the distance. From time to time he would call out. 'Hello. Hello.' And then we would listen. It was very still. Sounds carried. But no human voices did we hear. The caretaker looked cold in his shirt.

We were in there just over three hours when we heard a door open and shut close by. The caretaker began to call out again.

A voice said. 'Where are you?'

'In the Jews.'

'What are you doing there?'

'We can't get out.'

The bolt was drawn across. The green door opened. The two old men talked about the delinquency of children these days. That they showed no respect for their elders.

I walked away. Through the archway I could see the fine sweep of Mount's Bay, St Michael's Mount, the blue water, the fields, the coastline fading in the distance.

I know that with some people after someone has died they

want to tell as many others as they can about it, or start thinking of taking out life insurance, or wonder where they will be
buried. My reaction is to enter Emily. That night, in bed, it
seemed important to emphasize that we were alive.

Chapter Twenty-two

THE PHONE RANG.

'Hello,' I said.

'Hullo old boy.'

'Albert. Where are you?'

'In London, at the flat. Did you get a letter from me?'

'No. I didn't.'

'When it comes, don't act on it. I sent you a letter from Vienna. It will be interesting if they don't let the letter through.'

'Who?'

'I can't tell you over the phone. I've had some adventure.'

'When did you write the letter?'

'What day is it today?'

'The twenty-seventh.'

'No, what *day* is it?'

'Sunday.'

'I wrote it on Wednesday. But it may not have gone then. I know this is melodramatic but I can't tell you over the phone. When the letter comes let me know.'

Next morning I waited for the postman. No letter from Vienna. Neither the next day. I thought I'd probably not be able to read it anyway.

On the fourth day I had a letter from Albert. It was typed.

Dear Joseph,

It's all right. I found the letter I wrote to you. The fact is that I was arrested by the Austrian police and I was worried about something I had written. On this occasion my bad (illegible) hand-writing saved me and they didn't see it. Sorry to be so melodramatic. I'll tell you next time when I see you. Love to all.

Albert

On January 25th there was another phone call. 'Joseph?'

'Hello Albert.'

'Happy New Year.'

'Same to you.'

'Ich will nit sind dramatik aber du waist mir nicht. *Farsh-tait?*'

'Ich farshtai,' I said.

'Nobody has come around to ask about me, have they?'

'No.'

He sounded disappointed. 'Don't let them know that I live here.'

A week later I came up to London. I was curious about Albert. But I also wanted a few days in London. After ten unbroken months in Carnbray the sight of the water in the bay, the gulls, the front, just depress me. I need to be able to go out and walk down straight streets again and talk to someone, just talk.

Olga made tea and Albert and I sat opposite each other in the room surrounded by books, furniture, photographs.

'I'm a coward,' he said. 'I flunked it. Like I did before.'

'You tried before?' I said.

'At Frankfurt. But I was a coward then. And I was a coward now.'

He got up, closed the doors so Olga would not hear.

'I went to Austria. There was this man Apfel. He was responsible for getting Jews sent to concentration camps. I was supposed to get a gun at Southampton. But it didn't come. I had these bullets and a knife. I went to Vienna. Rented a car and drove out to Kreuze – I got the address from Letros – he keeps track of all the Nazis.

'I went to Kreuze – it's just a small agricultural village by a lake. I found the house. There wasn't anyone about.

'I tried again towards evening. I went around the back. This time I tried the back door. It was open. I went up the stairs. Rang the bell. A woman came to the door. A quite ordinary woman. I think it was seeing a woman ... She said, What do you want? I told her I was a British journalist wanting to interview Herr Apfel. Then I heard this strong voice call out from inside the house.

' "*Nein.*"

'She closed the door. I went down the stairs. I was a coward. I should have gone right in. I went back to the hotel and lay down. I was determined to try again tomorrow. I wrote you a letter saying that if you don't hear from me to get in touch with the family.

'I was lying down having a rest when there was a knock at the door. I said who is it, and it was the maid. As I opened the door five or six big men pushed me to the wall and searched me to see if I had a gun. They told me to get dressed and to come along. I said what for? They said they would tell me later.

'We all got into this black car. And this was happening right in the middle of Vienna. Here I was being driven. And there were the crowds walking by, some were shopping. Old boy, you have no idea what's going on in cars that just drive by.

'I was interrogated for three days. I stuck to my cover story. I told them I was writing a book.

'What kind of book, they asked.

'It's called *The Wondering Jew*. I wrote it out for them. It's a pun, I said. Wandering. Wondering.

' "Yah, Yah," they said.

'They wanted to know why I had all the bullets. Who was my accomplice? I told them a story that I wanted to go shooting in Czechoslovakia.

'They were all very correct. There was an older detective, at the back, looking down some glasses. He seemed friendly so I smiled at him. Then he came up and said. "Why are you laughing at me? Why are you making fun of me?"

'I was worried about the letter to you because I had Letros's name in it. After three days they said I could have a public trial or be deported for ten years. I was going to have a public trial and make a nuisance. But I decided in the end to be deported. I'm a coward. Don't you think I'm a coward?'

'We are all cowards about something,' I said, feeling uncomfortable.

He got up suddenly and walked to the table and wrote something down. 'I must earn some money. Sorry I won't be seeing much of you this time but Olga will look after you.'

After he left I asked Olga. 'How is he?'

'He is sick sir. Tell him to see a doctor. He quarrel with everybody – with his brothers.'

'But why?'

'Because they do not want to go to the cemetery. He have big fight. He ask them why don't they go to the cemetery every week. They say they don't want. He take them by the neck and carry them outside. Throw them out. He go every week. Spend pounds on flowers for the graves.'

'Is he working?'

'He reads books and calls that working. He send things out. But they all say no good or full up. It all come back. We go to Auschwitz. I tell Albert – you make a little article, you have pictures, you were there. Then we come back. Some weeks later there is someone else who write about Auschwitz with pictures. I say to him why didn't you? He is muddled sir. He sell the business. Now he has about nine thousand pounds. But what will happen in a year? He will be on the streets.'

'Nine thousand pounds will last him more than a year.'

'But he go with this woman. This rubbish. She stay all day in bed. You think he go to work in Soho. He got this woman up there.'

'Who is she?'

'Someone he know in the war. She leave her husband. They do not have much money. Albert give her money. She go and do expensive hair-do. And say to me. Olga. How do you like my hair? It's grey, I say. And Albert is angry. She say to me. How do you think my new frock is? I say, you're fat. And Albert is angry. I'm not going to give breakfast to this rubbish.*

I went to see Charles but he was not in. A new door was put on but I saw the top window had been broken leaving a large

---

I met her once at Albert's flat in Soho. Her name was Pat. A largish blonde with nice dark eyes. She reminded me of w.a.a.f.s and a.t.s. in the last war. She seemed anxious to please. After a few drinks she said. 'Would you like to see my imitations? This is my Alan Ladd. This is my Gary Cooper.' And even in her imitations she was dated. Five months later the Middle East war broke out. I wrote Albert wondering, as I did, if he hadn't already gone there. It seemed to be something that Albert had been waiting for all his life. And I was back to listening to the news on the radio, TV, the newspapers. When I didn't hear from him for three days I phoned. Olga answered. She said that Albert was in France 'with that woman'. Three weeks later Albert phoned. He was back in London. He sounded sad and disappointed. He said he was in France on an isolated farm. Had not known of the war. By the time he got back it was all over.

hole. I went to Blooms for a couple of meals. I walked along the streets. A woman looked at me as I crossed Piccadilly. For a moment I thought it was Anna. By the time I came back at night to the flat I was tired.

The telephone rang. It was Albert.

'Any telephone calls for me?'

'No,' I said.

'When are you going back?'

'Tomorrow morning – I'm catching the 10:30 at Paddington.'

'Let's have breakfast,' he said. 'I'll meet you outside the French pub.'

Next morning just before eight I was outside the York Minster and there was Albert. He brought me to a shabby dark café. We had cheese rolls and coffee full of chicory. I thought how sad it looked. But for Albert the place was full of sentiment. But then he was a sentimental man. He told me that everyone who was anybody used to come here during the 1940s. And when we came out he pointed to other drab restaurants, shabby doorways that meant nothing to me, and told me what they had once been.

An old man in a worn green tweed coat approached us. The coat was fastened together by a safety pin. 'Can you spare a few pennies for a cup of tea?'

'You're very naughty,' Albert said with a smile. And gave him a shilling. 'I'll end up like him,' he said, 'if I'm not careful.'

He looked, I thought, a happy man in a grey anorak with a fur collar, standing on the corner of Dean and Old Compton Streets, the wind blowing the remaining grey hair about.

'Give my love to Emily and the children,' he said. 'Children? They've probably all grown up. When they see me they'll say: who is that old man.'

Chapter Twenty-three

CHARLES RANG this morning. He'd like to come down for a few days. Could I get him a room 'for two'.

Immediate excitement and curiosity. And next morning I see him walking up the road with a young man in his late twenties that he introduced as Arthur.

At the start it was just like always with Charles telling us the people he's seen, about where he has been, what he has done. And Arthur sitting there quietly, dressed in a dark blue suit, white shirt, plain dark tie, and hair not crew cut but short. When he did speak he spoke with a cockney accent that he tried to cover up.

I walk them to the Riviera Hotel and once inside Charles takes over, signs the register, does the talking, while Arthur stands there quietly.

That night they came to take us out for dinner. 'Arthur likes Carnbray,' Charles said. 'I think we may stay a few days longer.'

'It's very nice,' Arthur said shyly.

After dinner we walked along the front. Arthur walked with Emily. And I with Charles. Charles tells me that he met Arthur at a party, that he was a bookie's clerk and came from Elephant and Castle. 'He's very nice,' Charles said.

The blue light at the end of the pier; the row of white lights on the other; and between, the cottages and houses lit up, from the inside, looking like pumpkins in the dark.

'As you see we're still here,' I said. 'I still think I'll get us out.'

'It doesn't really matter,' he said. 'You live your life out here just as well as anywhere else.'

From somewhere in the darkness on the rocks gulls were sounding.

'I'm fifty-four,' Charles said. 'Not long to go now. But painters as they get older do their best work.'

'Do you think often of death?'

'Every day.'

I asked him if he had seen Anna. I had read in the gossip column of one of the papers that she was in London to make a film.

'*Her*,' Charles said in disgust. 'She'll pick up anything. Negroes, queers. They had parts of her diary in a Continental movie magazine. "I woke this morning with the taste of semen still in my mouth" was the way it began.'

I thought how innocent we were.

We didn't see Charles and Arthur next day. But they turned up the day after with an orange Le Creuset pot for Emily. After they left I said, 'wasn't that a nice thing to do.'

'They must have been talking about us,' she said.

It was a slightly different Charles this time. He was more subdued.

'It's such a nice place, Carnbray,' Arthur said. 'I wish I had a camera.'

'I'll get you one when we get back,' Charles said.

Three months later it was Arthur who rang up. He thought he'd like to come down. He asked if I could get him a room in the same hotel. Which I did. He said Charles was painting and he couldn't get away.

Emily and I were up early, as usual, but without much enthusiasm. It was the wrong person coming down. Neither of us particularly wanted to see Arthur.

'He's late,' I said. 'It's half-past eight.'

At nine the phone rang. It was Arthur phoning from the railway station. He didn't know where we lived.

I told him.

'What shall I do with our case?'

'Leave it at the hotel then come down.'

'That's a good idea.'

He came and introduced us to a tall young boy with fair hair called Terry.

Emily made them bacon and eggs and tea.

'It was a terrible train ride. We got on just after ten last night and only now got in. Charles sends his love. He's working. He didn't want to come down. He's working for this show in Paris in a year's time.'

143

'How is he?'

'He doesn't go into pubs now. He doesn't like pubs any more. He sees very few people.'

I said I would walk them back to the hotel. And on the way met The Voice of Calcutta.

'This is Arthur and Terry,' I said.

'How do you do,' he said. 'Did I tell you about the two queers. They were standing back to back and they got the wind up.'

He laughed and went on his way.

I saw Arthur blush.

'He's silly,' I said.

At the hotel there was a noticeable difference. On his own Arthur didn't know what to do. He didn't have any kind of authority. I asked him if he wanted to go into a cheaper hotel. 'No,' he said. 'They were very nice before.'

They came to see us around eight and we went out for a drink. Terry said he liked Carnbray. Arthur said he liked it as well. But I mostly asked him questions about Charles.

'When he's working,' Arthur said, 'he drives himself to finish something. He really drives himself. And he keeps on sending me away with people. He buys the tickets. I've been all over.'

'Where were you last?'

'I went on a tour of the Middle East. Charles asked me if I'd like to go with this photographer he knew during the war. He bought the photographer new clothes, he bought our tickets, he gave us each a hundred pounds. But this man. You know what he does. He eats pound notes. He gave a girl a ten pound note. And she gave him seven pounds and some change. And he stood there eating the notes. He said they were tasteless.'

When Arthur went to get a round of drinks Terry said, 'He lives for Charles. They ring each other early in the morning, every day.'

'What does Arthur do?'

'When Charles is working – nothing. He spends a lot of time in Battersea Gardens. He goes to films. He has seen *The Sound of Music* eight times. Then comes evening he sees Charles and his day begins.'

Arthur came back with the drinks. 'You're very lucky,' he said, 'having Emily and the children.'

Next day they came early in the morning to borrow the surf-board to go surfing. I took them down to the beach. It was very funny. Arthur had never surfed before. I showed him how to hold the board. But he was going the wrong way. Instead of coming in with a wave. He was meeting the wave pointing to the sea. He was trying to surf out to sea. People were laughing. I said I would see them later.

They didn't call that day. I let it go the way I do when Charles is down. Let them make their own amusements. Perhaps they wanted to be on their own. The last thing Arthur said was that he liked it here and was going to stay ten days.

Next evening Terry came, all dressed up in a good suit.

'Would you and Emily like to come up to the hotel and have a drink with Arthur. He's now decided to leave tomorrow.'

'But why?' I asked.

'He's had trouble in the hotel. They won't do anything for him. They treat him like dirt. He wanted some laundry done. They wouldn't even consider until he gave them a big tip. They wouldn't shine his shoes. They don't take any notice of him.'

'What have you been doing the last two days?'

'He's been getting drunk on champagne. All the time. We've hardly been on the beach.'

We came to the hotel. Arthur was sitting by himself in the lounge beside the plate glass wall facing the bay, drinking champagne. It was very pretty outside. The time of evening when the sea is lighter than the sky. And the French Crabbers have just lit their lights.

'What took you so long,' he said blurring his words. 'Come and sit down. Let's have another bottle of champagne. Another bottle. They're so slow. They're not taking any notice of me.'

It was one of those English middle-class provincial hotels. Full of matronly women and red-faced men. Drinking sherry and bottled beer. And looking disapprovingly in our direction.

'I thought you liked it here,' I said. 'Why are you leaving so quickly.'

'There's nothing to do here,' Arthur said. 'There's no night life. We'll go on to Brighton. I'll send you a card.'

On to Brighton, as he had gone to Majorca, to Tangier, to Marseilles, to Cyprus, Monaco. And as Arthur drank he became more and more like the painting Charles had done of him. He was disintegrating in front of our eyes. And he spoke more Cockney than ever. I caught glimpses of all these middle-class people gazing unapprovingly at Arthur drinking, at the champagne, at Arthur drunk. I suddenly liked Arthur. The hell with them.

Terry was sitting beside me and opposite was Emily and Arthur.

'He's got this marvellous flat that Charles bought him,' Terry said. 'It's full of gadgets – but no food. Only milk.'

'Why are you all dressed up,' Arthur said. 'Why did you put on a suit and tie?'

'We put it on for you.'

'For us? We're just a couple of tramps.'

But he had drunk too much. And he decided to go upstairs. Terry went with him. We sat there with a half-bottle of champagne. When Terry came back I said I would come tomorrow to see them off.

I did get up early next morning. And joined Arthur and Terry at the breakfast table. 'I find I have picked up words from Charles,' he said. 'He always says terribly nice. Or they're terribly nice people. And I do it now.'

What he didn't realize was just how dependent he was on Charles. Being with Charles he had been taken to the large hotels. But without Charles, when he tried to do the same, it didn't come off. There were only the small humiliations.

'I had a leather briefcase from the gallery,' Arthur said. 'It said to Arthur for being the inspiration for so many paintings by Charles. Wasn't that nice?'

I said it was. I also said that we had seen a difference in Charles since they were together. Charles seemed settled.

'I'm very glad to hear it,' he said.

At the desk he went to pay the bill and there was a letter from Charles. It said that he was working well, sent his love, 'If you like it in Carnbray why don't you stay an extra week or even two. I hope you spend some time on the beach. The sun will do you good.'

We walked to the house to say goodbye to Emily and the children.

He began to take out some money. Emily began to say, 'Don't be silly Arthur —' She wanted to say don't be silly at Brighton. He thought it meant about wanting to give something to the children. Poor Arthur. Without Charles he was lost.

'What rent do you pay for this house?'

'Three pounds ten a week,' I said.

'That's what I pay my cleaning woman. You know Charles doesn't care. Money means nothing to him. Or things. But it does to me.' He saw our television set. 'That's nice. How much did you pay for it?'

'Seventy-five guineas.'

'You're lucky,' he said. 'You and Charles have got your work.'

It could have been Emily talking. Just as I thought of Emily last night when Arthur was talking about small humiliations at the hotel. I remembered the time she came back to say the grocer was rude to her, the man in the electric shop, the salesgirl at Woolworths. The time she told me that she said Hello to a woman, she had met some time ago, in the street. And the woman said, 'I'm afraid I don't know who you are.'

'I've got these lovely colours,' Arthur said, 'all in my head. But I'd never paint them. If I did they'd be no good. There's nothing to do but get drunk.' And Emily saying. 'The trouble with me is I can't do anything well.'

'You've had three kids.'

'Oh, anybody can do that,' she said contemptuously.

We got off the single-track train at the end of the branch line and walked to the other part of the platform along the windswept station and waited for the train to London.

'I suppose I won't see you for another six months or a year.' Arthur said.

'I suppose not,' I said.

'What a world,' he said.

'Who knows by that time we may have moved to Brighton. Will you come and see us in Brighton?'

'I'll be your first guest,' Arthur said.*

Next time in London I told Charles about Arthur's stay in Carnbray. 'They didn't take any notice of him at the hotel,' I said. 'He doesn't have any existence outside you.'

Charles was cynical. 'It would be better if he would go back where he came from.'

I couldn't tell him that it was now impossible for Arthur to go back. That Charles had made it so he could never go back.

'I have tried to get him to do things,' Charles said. 'But he won't finish anything. I was going to give a party for a friend I know. And Arthur said he was going to commit suicide.'

'Did you invite Arthur to the party?'

'Of course. I went over to his place to see. And he didn't even have the rope. I asked him how he was going to commit suicide without a rope. I have some money that I keep here. Arthur took the money then rang up to tell me he stole it.'

Seven months later Arthur killed himself.

Chapter Twenty-four

I REALIZE now that I have probably given a wrong impression of the kind of life we have lived in Carnbray. I've made it sound all more eventful than it really is. There are days that go by when nothing happens. When we have no one to come and see us for weeks or even longer. When no one rings on the phone. Then I might go and clear the drain in the courtyard and feel better. Or I might get up early and walk down to the front. The early morning scent from the roses and honey-suckle of the gardens down the road. And the fresh morning air, the sea's blue water, birds resting and flying, and the sense of a multitude of creatures living out their minute lives. But this is not enough.

'We need other people,' Emily said, 'to find out what we are like.'

Sometimes I come up here feeling depressed. The wind rattles the windows. Children's voices come from the play-ground. It's eleven – recess – and I sit here thinking why don't I end it all. Why go on? What a con-trick this business of looking after a wife and kids. I wonder what to write about to bring in some money. Maybe I wasn't cut out for 'the free life'. If you can call this kind of living free. Perhaps I'm in the wrong job. I could have been a professor in some provincial university in Canada. I would have books in shelves behind me. I would have a place to study and prepare my next lecture. An office and a secretary. Mimeographed bits of paper would be pushed underneath my door every day telling me what is going on. I'd have colleagues. A pay cheque at the end of each month. I'd go and have coffee and doughnuts in the faculty club at eleven. Sit in the dark leather chairs. Look out at a frozen landscape. Talk about a review, an article, or books, or gossip about people who were not there. Students I pass on the campus would say Hello. And people in town will show a certain respect. How I wish I was part of a community. Have some kind of role to play locally. I don't like this kind of indifference I have to the local newspaper here, the local goings on. There are times I feel I'm living like a criminal. Perhaps we're living like this because I'm no longer a travel writer. And this isolation is responsible for that change. Or maybe it was Emily. I remember how annoyed I was, earlier on, when Emily told other people that we were broke.

'I can't tell lies,' she said.

She had been talking with another housewife in the road. 'This coat will do for Ella. I don't know what we'll do for Martha.'

'Why do you go and talk to other people that we have no money,' I said. 'You have no right to talk to other people to tell them we're broke.'

'You can put it all in a story. But I have no right,' she said.

What could I say. I saw nothing wrong in writing about it because I saw writing as something different than living. I mean I tell the truth in writing. But in life I live it in different ways, with different people, full of evasions. But now it's 11:10 in the morning, the air-raid siren has sounded a fire, and Rebecca won't be home for another hour for lunch. As long as Emily hears the typewriter going she thinks I'm working. I put another sheet of paper in and type. Here it is a marvellous hot summer's day – and I'm up here writing about being miserable.

I think of a friend of Martha's. She's much more developed. And she's older, seventeen. I saw her coming back from school last week in her summer school dress. I think how nice it would be. I sit here thinking of that. Then I go and see Emily downstairs. She is in the kitchen.

'Come upstairs.'

'All right.'

I wonder if she will ask me what has made me randy all of a sudden. And what answer will I give. But she doesn't ask. She undresses. And there's no fooling about. It's over in ten minutes. And I come back up here.

Or the time I woke up at night and realized that Emily was lying on the pillow crying.

'What's wrong?'

'I can't go on,' she said.

'Why not?'

'Why can't you get us out of here.'

'We could go to Canada.'

'You know I'll never go there,' she said. 'Why can't you get us closer to London. I wouldn't mind Brighton. We could have the sea there too. And London is only an hour by train.'

'I'll try,' I said.

'I had a dream,' she said. 'We were on a pier – at least I and the children – then I realized the pier was sinking. And it was getting black. And we were all going under. I woke up and I was crying.'

I kissed her cheek.

'I can't stand it here any more. No one comes to see us. We have no friends. I can't go on depending on a phone call from London to say Charles is coming down.'

'I'll try and work something out,' I said.

'This isn't just you saying things as you always do to please me?'

'No, I will do something,' I said. And she went to sleep very quickly.

Chapter Twenty-five

WE HAVE LIVED in Carnbray twelve years.* I have grown older and don't talk as much as I used to. Martha has gone off to London to a college, she wants to teach English. Ella and Rebecca are still at school here. Anna is still in Hollywood. Sometimes one of her films comes on in one of the local cinemas. I look at the stills outside but I don't go in. Once I stood to be weighed on the large weighing machine outside the bus station. The card that came out, giving my weight and fortune, had a picture of Anna on the back: 'No 3 in a series of film stars – Anna Likely'. Charles lives in Switzerland. Whenever he has a new show I see colour reproductions in the colour supplements. I haven't been up to London for over two years. The last time I saw Albert he was waiting for a letter. When it came he held it unopened in his hand and said. 'I applied for a job, to be assistant editor of *The History of the Twentieth Century*. I hope I don't get it. I was interviewed. And all the time I thought. Do I want to do this? Of course not.' He opened the letter. 'Well, that's that. I didn't get it. It's as if fate was deciding things for me.' The grass in front of the house of the spinster down the road is overgrown. I have not seen her for months. Just as the Russian lady is no longer to be seen walking along the front. Nor The Voice of Calcutta. People disappear. And that's that. Life seems to be a series of unconnected brief encounters.

When I go out in the street some older people in Carnbray take off their hats and say 'Good morning sir.' I now write nothing but short stories. They get published here and in Canada. And from this I average £1500 a year. We don't drive a car. But we pay our bills on time. And I smoke cigars, long thin Dutch ones.

I haven't been to Canada for six years. Although I still have the two wrist watches going on my desk with one set at the time over there. Mother writes about once a month. 'Nothing

---

*And it is twenty years since that first summer with the Captains, the Majors, the Squadron Leaders ...

new around here' appears in all her letters. Sometimes she mentions Mona and Oscar. Oscar has had a heart attack and is unable to work but sits by the window doing jig-saw puzzles. Mona works in a small dress shop in Meridian. Their eldest daughter is a nurse.

I now don't mind if Emily leaves the toothpaste tops off – the jam jars at the edge. Maybe she does it less. It doesn't matter. I look at these things now as part of my own life. Emily still has hopes of getting away from here. She keeps on looking in *The Times* for rented properties. Then goes to the library, to a reference book showing all the counties of England, and looks up to see where these properties are. On Sundays she gets me out for walks with Ella and Rebecca. Up around the large houses and the hotels, the small wood, to the moors with the wild flowers and green fields. 'Just so we'll have nice pictures to take with us,' she said. She has also started to see signs in various things. She told me about this French Crabber that she saw in the bay. Most of the French Crabbers have gone for the winter and there are only these two. One is the usual two shades of green. But the other one is a brilliant red. She has never seen one like it before. Neither have I. She goes down regularly at teatime to see it come in. She sees all kinds of significance in this boat.

'I know it doesn't belong here. It looks so gay. And I know that one day I'll go down. And it will be gone.

'I like that thought,' she said.

About the author

NORMAN LEVINE was born in Ottawa in 1923. During World War II, he served in the RCAF with a Lancaster squadron based in Yorkshire. He subsequently studied at Cambridge and McGill Universities, receiving his M.A. from McGill University in 1949. In 1949 he was awarded a $5,000 fellowship to do post-graduate work at King's College, London. He left Canada with the manuscript for his first novel under his arm and spent the next thirty-one years in England, mainly in St Ives, Cornwall. He returned to Canada briefly in 1965-66 when he was the first writer-in-residence at the University of New Brunswick.

Norman Levine is the author of two books of poetry, *Myssium* (1948) and *The Tightrope Walker* (1950); two novels, *The Angled Road* (1952) and *From a Seaside Town* (1970); and several collections of short fiction, including *One Way Ticket* (1961), *Canada's Winter Tales* (1968), *I don't want to know anyone too well* (1971), *Selected Stories* (1975), *Thin Ice* (1979), *Why do you live so far away?* (1984), *Champagne Barn* (1984) and *Something Happened Here* (1991). His stories have been translated and published throughout Europe.

In 1980 Levine returned to Canada. He currently lives and works in France.